ACCLAIM FOR
JIM THOMPSON

"The best suspense writer going, bar none." —*New York Times*

"My favorite crime novelist—often imitated but never duplicated." —Stephen King

"My man in crime fiction." —Jo Nesbø

"If Raymond Chandler, Dashiell Hammett, and Cornell Woolrich would have joined together in some ungodly union and produced a literary offspring, Jim Thompson would be it.... His work casts a dazzling light on the human condition." —*Washington Post*

"The master of the American groin-kick novel." —*Vanity Fair*

"Like Clint Eastwood's pictures it's the stuff for rednecks, truckers, failures, psychopaths, and professors.... One of the finest American writers and the most frightening, Thompson is on best terms with the devil. Read Jim Thompson and take a tour of hell." —*New Republic*

"The most hard-boiled of all the American writers of crime fiction." —*Chicago Tribune*

BOOKS BY JIM THOMPSON

The Alcoholics
A Swell-Looking Babe
After Dark, My Sweet
Bad Boy
The Criminal
Cropper's Cabin
The Getaway
The Golden Gizmo
The Grifters
Heed the Thunder
A Hell of a Woman
The Killer Inside Me
The Kill-Off
The Nothing Man
Nothing More than Murder
Now and on Earth
Pop. 1280
Recoil
The Rip-Off
Roughneck
Savage Night
South of Heaven
Texas by the Tail
The Transgressors
Wild Town

SAVAGE NIGHT

JIM THOMPSON

Foreword by Mark Winegardner

MULHOLLAND BOOKS

LITTLE, BROWN AND COMPANY

NEW YORK BOSTON LONDON

Copyright © 1953 by Jim Thompson, copyright © renewed 1981 by Alberta H. Thompson
Foreword copyright © 2014 by Mark Winegardner
Excerpt from *Now and on Earth* copyright © 1942 by Jim Thompson, copyright © renewed 1970 by The Estate of Jim Thompson

Mulholland Books / Little, Brown and Company
Hachette Book Group
237 Park Avenue, New York, NY 10017
mulhollandbooks.com

Originally published in paperback by Lion Books, October 1953
First Mulholland Books paperback edition, August 2014

Mulholland Books is an imprint of Little, Brown and Company, a division of Hachette Book Group, Inc. The Mulholland Books name and logo are trademarks of Hachette Book Group, Inc.

The publisher is not responsible for websites (or their content) that are not owned by the publisher.

Library of Congress Cataloging-in-Publication Data

Thompson, Jim, 1906–1977.
  Savage night / Jim Thompson; foreword by Mark Winegardner.—First Mulholland Books paperback edition.
    pages cm
    ISBN 978-0-316-40382-5 (paperback)—ISBN 978-0-316-19610-9 (ebook)
1. Assassins—Fiction. I. Title.
  PS3539.H6733S2 2014
  813'.54—dc23   2014015911

10 9 8 7 6 5 4 3 2 1

Printed in the United States of America

FOREWORD

Jim Thompson always knew how to get things started, and his bewitching and peculiar *Savage Night* commences with the confidence of a pro. Our hard-bitten narrator (a hired killer, we'll soon learn) steps off a train in a nowheresville by the name of Peardale. In service to someone in New York known only as "The Man," he's come to kill. He's come from far away—somewhere west of Chicago. The "slight cold" he contracted in the Windy City has been fed by three days of the suitably noirish afflictions of "babes and booze" in New York. *Of course* he arrives hungover. But then, "for the first time in years," he spits blood.

We expect our pulp (anti-)heroes to show up dissipated, but *tubercular?*

We expect gritty, urban mean streets. Or sun-baked, decadent California boulevards. Or even a violent, hardscrabble town in the dusty remains of the American frontier. What the hell are we doing a hundred miles from NYC, in Peardale, Long Island, a "decayed, dying-on-the-vine" burg with no economy but "the farm trade" and a diploma-mill teachers college? As

Charlie "Little" Bigger lugs his two suitcases up the main drag, he sizes up Peardale and decides (more accurately than he knows) that it's the personification of a middle-aged loser's hapless comb-over.

What we have here is the story of a fish-out-of-water in the boondocks, right? And so we *certainly* expect him to be yearning to get back to the bright lights of some big city. If not New York or L.A., then Detroit. Chicago. Philly, worst case. Nope. Though the locals will soon take to calling him a "slicker," Charlie, instead, longs to be "back at the filling station in Arizona."

Naturally, we expect Charlie Bigger to be—like most pulp protagonists, even in most other Jim Thompson novels—physically tough and probably a ladykiller, a blithe mercenary who is confident (probably overly so) and smart enough to be one step ahead of the other characters at (nearly) every turn.

Charlie, yes, comes off, for the most part, like a guy who's got it all figured out. But his narration is unreliable, and his confidence never runs as deep as he'd like us to believe. He's frankly paranoid. His anxiety that he's not outsmarting anyone but himself seeps through the cracks in his sociopathic facade. And, sure, he's in Peardale to do a $30,000 job, but the prospect of that payday (a quarter-million bucks in today's dollars) is, for Charlie, just a joyless and possibly quixotic alternative to becoming "no me, no nothing." As for physically tough? Charlie Bigger—even with lifts in his shoes—stands just five feet tall.

Foreword

The first time Charlie describes himself to us—or, rather, describes his reflection in the window of a Peardale shoe store—he does so mostly with vague, aw-shucks details ("I wasn't much to look at," "I didn't add up to much") that come off as likably self-deprecating. Then, when he walks into the store to buy himself a pair of shoes, the owner can't stop himself from calling Charlie "sonny," which Charlie finds condescending and which further skews our sympathies his way.

Because of his size (plus his newly acquired contact lenses, and newly fixed-up teeth, not to mention the healthy tan he got in Arizona, where, we intuit, he's been warding off his TB for "years"), Charlie comes off as much younger than he is. Only up close do people see that he's a middle-aged, dead-eyed wreck.

The owner (who will also disappear from the novel after this scene) becomes the first of many characters who seem to accept at face value that Charlie's who he says he is—an earnest, humbly dressed young fella named Carl Bigelow who's about to start classes at the teachers college—because it enables their own ends. In the owner's case, this is both the sale of a pair of size 5AA elevator shoes and, more so, the pleasant delusion that he's a local sage imparting his wisdom about Peardale and its peccadillos to a naive and grateful lad.

Charlie feels like he's being addressed as "an idiot child," and yet he plays along. He pretends to be surprised to learn that the J. C. Winroy, who owns the boardinghouse where he's arranged to stay, is none other than *the* Jake Winroy, a barbershop owner/bookie who'd worked his way up to being entrusted by the "big boys" (none bigger than The Man) to deliver bribes to judges and politicians so they'd ignore an illegal horse-betting racket. When Winroy got busted, he refused to name names. But after nine months in prison, he couldn't take it anymore, agreed to turn state's evidence, and was released, pending trial.

Charlie feigns alarm at all this, though of course he's here to execute Winroy. He needs to stay at the boardinghouse long enough that he won't arouse suspicion and then make it look like an accident, so that it'll be impossible to pin it on The Man.

The store owner reassures Charlie that, despite everything, it'd be fine to stay at the Winroys' house. There's another boarder—a baker named Kendall: a nice older gentleman. Sure, the joint's rundown, but there's a sweet one-legged girl, a college student named Ruthie, who doesn't live there but who comes around to help cook and clean. And there's *Mrs.* Winroy, who hates her husband's sorry guts and—nudge nudge, wink wink—might just be a "stepper." In the world of Jim Thompson, even a goody-goody busybody like the store owner might at any moment shift gears and goad a supposed innocent toward depravity.

Charlie feigns embarrassment. Fucking Fay Winroy, though, was already part of the plan.

And we're off. Off to the races. Off any notion that the novel is going to be content with laying down genre expectations without also subverting them. Familiar *enough* but never entirely familiar. We will occasionally rocket off the rails, into flights of inscrutable, thrilling fancy and madness, in passages that evoke comparisons with William S. Burroughs or Philip K. Dick. Not for nothing do the Coen brothers cite Jim Thompson as an influence. There are two infamous, profane, and hallucinatory set pieces in *Savage Night* in which an unhinged, benevolent writer much like Jim Thompson launches himself on a word-drunk crazy-prophet rant—scenes entirely of a piece with John Goodman's roles in *O Brother Where Art Thou?* and *Barton Fink.*

None of which is to slight the novel's main story line, which is as taut, nasty, and resourceful as any Thompson ever created.

Jake Winroy turns out, unexpectedly, to be a kind of ominous near-absence, a drunken, dying sun around which the other principal characters revolve.

Fay Winroy hates her husband, sure, but what's in it for *her* to tumble into bed with Charlie? He's no ladykiller (at least not in the colloquial sense of that). He's not even an especially charming sociopath. If this were a novel by the great James M. Cain, we'd expect that Fay's so eager to see Jake die that she's willing to sleep with a man to manipulate him into doing the deed. But Charlie's *already* here to kill Jake. There's no money left for Fay to inherit. Somehow, "stepping out" with Charlie feels believable as it develops (perhaps, dear reader, no more or less capricious than your own strangest assignation); still, we keep reading, braced for the other elevator shoe to drop.

Kindly old Kendall used to teach at the college but is no longer there, for reasons never revealed—and are we to read something into the quiet pulse of homosexual attraction his mentoring of "Carl" gives off? Why does Kendall stay in this crummy place at all? Might he be in league with The Man?

And, Jesus: Ruthie. I don't want to even get started on the warped complexities of Ruthie, except to tease you with this: you're never going to be able to unsee what you see in your mind's eye when her stump is unveiled.

As for Charlie "Little" Bigger—he's not merely a hitman but, as a true-crime magazine he carries around calls him, "the deadliest, most elusive killer in criminal history." He's known as Little Bigger because his now-dead older brother was called Big Luke Bigger. Big arranged the killings and Little did the jobs. Nobody in the underworld, supposedly, ever laid eyes on Little. There are no known pictures of him. He hasn't been heard from in, well, "years" and is widely presumed dead. Charlie's backstory just gets more warped and inventive (and oddly convincing) from there. And the novel keeps revealing him through his reflections—in mirrors, yes, but also in things like his portrayal in that magazine the contradictory tales Peardale's surprisingly competent sheriff coaxes (via letters and phone calls) from people back in Arizona. Each time, there's the sense of there being less and less of him, a metaphor Charlie "Little" Bigger seems to increasingly regard as nightmarishly literal.

Foreword

Ultimately, *Savage Night,* as you'll soon see, isn't so much a glimpse behind a psychopath's mask of sanity as a howling declaration that there *is* no mask. Stop averting your eyes! Evil and duplicity lie in plain sight, concealed by nothing but a lousy comb-over.

—Mark Winegardner

SAVAGE NIGHT

I

I'd caught a slight cold when I changed trains at Chicago; and
three days in New York—three days of babes and booze while I
waited to see The Man—hadn't helped it any. I felt lousy by the
time I arrived in Peardale. For the first time in years, there was a
faint trace of blood in my spit.

I walked through the little Long Island Railway station, and
stood looking up the main street of Peardale. It was about four
blocks long, splitting the town into two ragged halves. It ended
at the teachers' college, a half-dozen red brick buildings scat-
tered across a dozen acres or so of badly tended campus. The
tallest business building was three stories. The residences looked
pretty ratty.

I started coughing a little, and lighted a cigarette to quiet it. I
wondered whether I could risk a few drinks to pull me out of
my hangover. I needed them. I picked up my two suitcases and
headed up the street.

It was probably partly due to my mood, but the farther I got
into Peardale the less I liked it. The whole place had a kind of
decayed, dying-on-the-vine appearance. There wasn't any local

industry apparently; just the farm trade. And you don't have commuters in a town ninety-five miles from New York City. The teachers' college doubtless helped things along a little, but I figured it was damned little. There was something sad about it, something that reminded me of bald-headed men who comb their side hair across the top.

I walked a couple blocks without sighting a bar, either on the main drag or the side streets. Sweating, trembling a little inside, I set the suitcases down and lighted another cigarette. I coughed some more. I cursed The Man to myself, calling him every kind of a son-of-a-bitch I could think of.

I'd have given everything I had just to be back at the filling station in Arizona.

But it couldn't be that way. It was either me and The Man's thirty grand, or no me, no nothing.

I'd stopped in front of a store, a shoe store, and as I straightened I caught a glimpse of myself in the window. I wasn't much to look at. You could say I'd improved a hundred per cent in the last eight or nine years, and you wouldn't be lying. But I still didn't add up to much. It wasn't that my kisser would stop clocks, understand, or anything like that. It was on account of my size. I looked like a boy trying to look like a man. I was just five feet tall.

I turned away from the window, then turned back again. I wasn't supposed to have much dough, but I didn't need to be rolling in it to wear good shoes. New shoes had always done something for me. They made me feel like something, even if I couldn't look it. I went inside.

There was a little showcase full of socks and garters up near the front, and a chubby middle-aged guy, the proprietor, I guess, was bending over it reading a newspaper. He barely glanced up at me, then jerked his thumb over his shoulder.

"Right up the street there, sonny," he said. "Those red brick buildings you see."

"What?" I said. "I—"

"That's right. You just go right on up there, and they'll fix you up. Tell you what boarding house to go to and anything else you need to know."

"Look," I said. "I—"

"You do that, sonny."

If there's anything I don't like to be called, it's sonny. If there's a goddamned thing in the world I don't like to be called, it's sonny. I swung the suitcases high as I could and let them drop. They came down with a jar that almost shook the glasses off his nose.

I walked back to the fitting chairs and sat down. He followed me, red-faced and hurt-looking, and sat down on the stool in front of me.

"You didn't need to do that," he said, reproachfully. "I'd watch that temper if I were you."

He was right; I was going to have to watch it. "Sure," I grinned. "It just kind of gets my goat to be called sonny. You probably feel the same way when people call you fatty."

He started to scowl, then shifted it into a laugh. He wasn't a bad guy, I guess. Just a nosy know-it-all small-towner. I asked for size five double-A elevators, and he began dragging the job out to get in as many questions as possible.

Was I going to attend the teachers' college? Wasn't I entering a little late in the term? Had I got myself a place to stay yet?

I said that I'd been delayed by sickness, and that I was going to stay at the J.C. Winroy residence.

"Jake Winroy's!" He looked up sharply. "Why you don't—why are you staying there?"

"Mainly because of the price," I said. "It was the cheapest place for board and room the college had listed."

"Uh-huh," he nodded, "and do you know why it's cheap, son—young man? Because there ain't no one else that will stay there."

I let my mouth drop open. I sat staring at him, worried-looking. "Gosh," I said. "You don't mean he's *that* Winroy?"

"Yes, sir!" He bobbed his head triumphantly. "That's just who he is, the very same! The man who handled the payoff for that big horse-betting ring."

"Gosh," I said again. "Why I thought he was in jail!"

He smiled at me pityingly. "You're way behind the times, s—what'd you say your name was?"

"Bigelow. Carl Bigelow."

"Well, you're way behind on your news, Carl. Jake's been out for—well—six-seven months now. Got pretty sick of jail, I reckon. Just couldn't take it even if the big boys were paying him plenty to stay there and keep his mouth shut."

I kept on looking worried and kind of scared.

"Understand, now, I'm not saying that you won't be perfectly all right there at the Winroy place. They've got one other boarder—not a student, a fellow that works over to the

6

bakery—and he seems to do all right. There hasn't been a detective around the house in weeks."

"Detectives!" I said.

"Sure. To keep Jake from being killed. Y'see, Carl"—he spelled it out for me, like someone talking to an idiot child—"Y'see Jake is the key witness in that big bookie case. He's the only one who can put the finger on all them crooked politicians and judges and so on who were taking bribes. So when he agrees to turn state's evidence and they let him out of jail, the cops are afraid he might get killed."

"D-did—" My voice shook; talking with this clown was doing me a lot of good. It was all I could do to keep from laughing. "Did anyone ever try it?"

"Huh-uh...Stand up a minute, Carl. Feel okay? Well, let's try the other shoe...Nope, no one ever tried it. And the more you think about it, the easier it is to see why. The public just ain't much interested in seeing those bookies prosecuted, as things stand now. They can't see why it's so wrong to bet with a bookie when it's all right to bet at the track. But taking bets is one thing, and murder is another. The public wouldn't go for that, and o'course everyone'd know who was responsible. Them bookies would be out of business. There'd be such a stink the politicians would *have* to stage a cleanup, no matter how they hated to."

I nodded. He'd hit the nail right on the head. Jake Winroy couldn't be murdered. At least he couldn't be murdered in a way that looked like murder.

"What do you think will happen, then?" I said. "They'll just let Ja—Mr. Winroy go ahead and testify?"

"Sure," he snorted, "if he lives long enough. They'll let him testify when the case comes to trial—forty or fifty years from now... Want to wear 'em?"

"Yeah. And just throw the old ones away," I said.

"Yep, that's the way it's working out. Stalling. Getting the case postponed. They've already done it twice, and they'll keep right on doing it. I'd be willing to bet a hundred dollars that the case never does get into court!"

He'd have lost his money. The trial was set for three months from now, and it wouldn't be postponed.

"Well," I said, "that's the way it goes, I guess. I'm glad you think it'll be all right for me to stay with the Winroys."

"Sure," he winked at me. "Might even have yourself a little fun. Mrs. Winroy is quite a stepper—not that I'm saying anything against her, understand."

"Of course not," I said. "Quite a—uh—stepper, huh?"

"Looks like she could be, anyways, if she had the chance. Jake married her after he left here and moved to New York—after he was riding high, wide and handsome. It must be quite a comedown for her, living like she has to now."

I moved up to the front of the store with him to get my change.

I turned left at the first corner, and walked down an unpaved side street. There were no houses on it, only the rear end of the corner business building on one side of the alley, and a fenced in backyard on the other. The sidewalk was a narrow, rough-brick path, but it felt good under my feet. I felt taller, more on even terms with the world. The job didn't look so lousy any more. I hadn't wanted it and I still didn't. But now it was mostly because of Jake.

The poor bastard was kind of like me. He hadn't been anything, but he'd done his damnedest to be something. He'd pulled out of this hick town, and got himself a barber's job in New York. It was the only work he knew—the only thing he knew anything about—so he'd done that. He'd got himself into exactly the right shop, one down around City Hall. He'd played up to exactly the right customers, laughing over their corny jokes, kissing their tails, making them trust him. When the smashup came, he hadn't swung a razor in years and he was handling a million-dollar-a-month payoff.

The poor bastard, no looks, no education, no nothing—and he'd pulled himself up to the top. And now he was back on the bottom again. Running the one-chair barber shop he'd started with, trying to make a little dough out of the Winroy family residence that was too run-down to sell.

All the jack he'd made in the rackets was gone. The state had latched on to part of it and the federal government had taken another big bite, and lawyers had eaten up the rest. All he had was his wife, and the dope was that he couldn't get a kind word out of her, let alone anything else.

I walked along thinking about him, feeling sorry for him; and I didn't really notice the big black Cadillac pulled up at the side of the street nor the man sitting in it. I was just about to pass on by when I heard a, *"Psst!"* and I saw that it was Fruit Jar.

I dropped the suitcases, and stepped off the curb.

"You stupid pissant," I said. "What's the idea?"

"Temper." He grinned at me, his eyes narrowing. "What's *your* idea, sonny? Your train got in an hour ago."

I shook my head, too sore to answer him. I knew The Man hadn't put him on me. If The Man had been afraid of a runout, I wouldn't have been here.

"Beat it," I said. "Goddam you, if you don't get out of town and stay out, I will."

"Yeah? What do you think The Man will say about that?"

"You tell him," I said. "Tell him you drove down here in a circus wagon and stopped me on the street."

He wet his lips, uneasily. I lighted a cigarette, dropped the package into my pocket and brought my hand out. I slid it along the back of the seat.

"Nothing to get excited about," he mumbled. "You'll get into the city Saturday? The Man'll be back, and — *oof!*"

"That's a switchblade," I said. "You've got about an eighth of an inch in your neck. Like to have a little more?"

"You crazy bas — *oof!*"

I laughed and let the knife drop down upon the seat.

"Take it with you," I said. "I've been meaning to throw it away. And tell The Man I'll look forward to seeing him."

He cursed me, ramming the car into gear. He took off so fast I had to jump back to keep from going with him.

Grinning, I went back to the walk.

I'd been waiting for an excuse to hand one to Fruit Jar. Right from the beginning, when he'd first made contact with me in Arizona, he'd been picking at me. I hadn't done anything to him—but right away he was riding me, calling me kid, and sonny. I wondered what was behind it.

Fruit Jar needed dough like a boar hog needs tits. He'd dropped out of the bootleg racket before the war and gone into used cars. Now he was running lots in Brooklyn and Queens; he was making more money legit—if you can call used cars legit—than he'd ever made with the booze.

But if he hadn't wanted to come in, why was he coming in so much farther than he had to? He hadn't needed to come down here today. In fact, The Man wasn't going to like it a bit. So…So?

I was still thinking when I reached the Winroy residence.

2

If you've been around the East much, you've seen a lot of houses like it. Two stories high but looking a lot taller because they're so narrow in depth; steep-roofed with a chimney at each end and a couple of gabled attic windows about halfway down. You could gold-plate them and they'd look like hell, but they're usually painted in colors that make them look twice as bad as they normally would. This one was a crappy green with puke-brown trimming.

I almost stopped feeling sorry for Winroy when I saw it. A guy who would live in a place like that had it coming to him. You know — maybe I'm a little nuts on the subject — you know, there's just no sense to things like that. I'd bought a little shack in Arizona, but it sure didn't stay a shack long. I painted it an ivory white with a blue trim, and I did the window frames with a bright red varnish. . . . Pretty? It was like one of those pictures you see on Christmas cards.

. . . I pushed the sagging gate open. I climbed the rickety steps to the porch, and rang the bell. I rang it a couple of times, listening to it ring inside, but there wasn't any answer. I couldn't hear anyone stirring around.

I turned and glanced around the bare yard—*too goddamned lazy to plant a little grass.* I looked at the paint-peeled fence with half the pickets knocked off. Then my eyes came up and I looked across the street, and I saw her.

I couldn't let on, but I knew who she was. Even in a jersey and jeans, her hair pulled back in a horse's tail. She was standing in the door of a little bar down the street, not sure whether I was worth bothering with.

I went back down the steps and through the gate, and she started hesitantly across the street.

"Yes?" she called, while she was still several steps away. "Can I help you?" She had one of those husky well-bred voices—voices that are trained to sound well bred. One look at that frame of hers, and you knew the kind of breeding she'd had: straight out of Beautyrest by box-springs. One look at her eyes, and you knew she could call you more dirty words than you'd find in a mile of privies.

"I'm looking for Mr. or Mrs. Winroy," I said.

"Yes? I'm Mrs. Winroy."

"How do you do?" I said. "I'm Carl Bigelow."

"Yes?" That broad-A yes was getting on my nerves. "Should that mean something to me?"

"That depends," I said, "on whether fifteen dollars a week means anything to you."

"Fif—Oh, of *course!*" She laughed suddenly. "I'm terribly

sorry, Car—Mr. Bigelow. Our hired girl—our maid, that is—had to go home to her folks—a family crisis of some kind—and we were really expecting you last week and—and things have been in such a turmoil that—"

"Surely. Of course—" I cut her off. I hated to see anyone work so hard for a few bucks. "It's my fault, entirely. Can I make up for it by buying you a drink?"

"Well, I *was*—" She hesitated, doubtfully, and I began to like her a little better. "If you're sure you—"

"I can," I said. "Today's a celebration. Tomorrow I'll start tightening up."

"Well," she said, "in that case—"

I bought her two drinks. Then, because I could see she wanted to ask for it, I gave her thirty dollars.

"Two weeks in advance," I said. "Okay?"

"Oh, now," she protested, huskily, that well-bred voice hitting on all cylinders. "That's entirely unnecessary. After all—we—Mr. Winroy and I aren't doing this for money. We felt it was more or less our duty, you know, living here in a college town to—"

"Let's be friends," I said.

"Friends? I'm afraid I don't—"

"Sure. So we can relax. I hadn't been in town more than fifteen minutes before I knew all about Mr. Winroy's trouble."

Her face had gotten a little stiff. "I wish you'd told me," she said. "You must have thought I was a terrible fool to—"

"Will you," I said, "relax?" And I gave her my best grin, big and boyish and appealing. "If you keep talking about being in turmoil and a terrible fool and all that stuff, you'll get me dizzy. And I'm dizzy enough just looking at you."

She laughed. She gave my hand a squeeze. "Listen to the man! Or did you mean that the right way?"

"You know how I meant it," I said.

"I'll bet I look a fright. Honest to Hannah, Carl, I—Oop, listen to me. Calling you Carl, already."

"Everybody does," I said. "I wouldn't know how to take it if anyone called me mister."

But I'd like to try, I thought. And I'd sure try to take it.

"It's been such a mess, Carl. For months I couldn't open a door without a cop or a reporter popping out at me, and then just when I think it's finished and I'm going to have a little peace, it starts all over again. I don't like to complain, Carl—I really don't—but—"

She did like to, naturally. Everyone does. But a dame who'd lived on the soft money so long was too smart to do it.

She let her hair down just far enough to be friendly.

"That's certainly tough," I said. "How long do you plan on staying here?"

"How long?" She laughed shortly. "The rest of my life it looks like."

"You don't mean that," I said. "A woman like you."

"Why don't I mean it? What else can I do? I let everything slide when I married Jake. Gave up my singing—you knew I was a singer?—well, I gave that up. I haven't been in a night club in years except to buy a drink. I just let everything slide, my voice, my contacts; everything. Now, I'm not a kid any more."

"Now stop that," I said. "You stop that right now."

"Oh, I'm not complaining, Carl. Really I'm not...How about another drink?"

I let her buy it.

"Well," I said, "I don't know too much about the case, and it's easy for me to talk. But—"

"Yes?"

"I think Mr. Winroy should have stayed in jail. That's what I'd have done."

"Of course, you would! Any *man* would."

"But maybe he knows best," I said. "He'll probably work out some big deal that'll put you higher on the heap than you were before."

She turned her head sharply, her eyes blazing fire. But I was all wide-eyed and innocent.

The fire died, and she smiled and squeezed my hand again.

"It's sweet of you to say that, Carl, but I'm afraid...I get so damned burned up I—well, what's the use talking when I can't *do* anything?"

I sighed and started to buy another drink.

"Let's not," she said. "I know you can't afford it—and I've had enough. I'm kind of funny that way, I guess. If there's anything that gets me, it's to see a person keep pouring it down after they've had enough."

"You know," I said, "it's funny that you should mention that. It's exactly the way I feel. I can take a drink or even three or four, but then I'm ready to give it a rest. With me it's the companionship and company that counts."

16

"Of course. Certainly," she nodded. "That's the way it should be."

I picked up my change, and we left the place. We crossed the street, and I got my bags off the porch and followed her to my room. She was acting a little thoughtful.

"This looks fine," I said. "I'm sure I'm going to like it here."

"Carl—" She was looking at me, curiously, friendly enough but curious.

"Yes?" I said. "Is there something wrong?"

"You're a lot older than you look, aren't you?"

"Now, how old would that be?" And, then, I nodded soberly. "I must have tipped you off," I said. "You'd never have known it from looking at me."

"Why do you say it that way? You don't like—"

I shrugged. "What's the use not liking it? Sure, I love it. Who wouldn't like being a man and looking like a kid? Having people laugh every time you act like a man."

"I haven't laughed at you, Carl."

"I haven't given you the chance," I said. "Suppose things had been different. Suppose, say, I'd met you at a party and I'd tried to kiss you like any man in his right mind would. Why, you'd have laughed your head off! And don't tell me you wouldn't, because I know you would!"

I jammed my hands into my pockets and turned my back on her. I stood there, head bowed, shoulders slumped, staring down at the threadbare carpet...It was raw, corny as hell—but it had almost always worked before, and I was pretty sure it would with her.

She crossed the room and came around in front of me. She put a hand under my chin and tilted it up.

"You know what you are?" she said, huskily. "You're a slicker."

She kissed me on the mouth. "A slicker," she repeated, smiling at me slant-eyed. "What's a fast guy like you doing at a tank-town teacher's college?"

"I don't really know," I said. "It's hard to put into words. It's—well, maybe you know how it is. You've been doing the same thing for a long time, and you don't think you're getting ahead fast enough. So you look around for some way of changing things. And you're probably so fed up with what you've been doing that anything that comes along looks good to you."

She nodded. She knew how that was.

"I've never made much money," I said, "and I figured a little education might help. This was cheap, and it sounded good in the catalogues. At that, I almost got right back on the train when I saw what it looked like."

"Yes," she said, grimly, "I know what you mean. But—you are going to give it a try, aren't you?"

"I kind of think I will," I said. "Now, will you tell me something?"

"If I can."

"Are those real?"

"Those? What—Oh," she said, and laughed softly. "Boy, *are* we slick!...Wouldn't you like to know, though?"

"Well?"

"Well—" She leaned forward, suddenly. Eyes dancing, watching my face, she moved her shoulders from side to side, up and down. And then she stepped back quickly, laughing, holding me away with her hands.

"Huh-uh. No, sir, Carl! I don't know why—I must be losing my mind to let you get away with that much."

"Just so you don't lose anything else," I said, and she laughed again.

It was louder and huskier than any of the others. It was like those laughs you hear late at night in a certain type of saloon. You know. The people are all in a huddle at one end of the bar, and they're all looking at this one guy, their lips pulled back a little from their teeth, their eyes kind of glassy; and all at once his voice rises, and he slaps his hand down on the counter. And you hear the laughter.

"Sweet"—she gave me another quick pat on the cheek—"just as sweet as he can be. Now, I've got to get downstairs and throw something together for dinner. It'll be about an hour from now in case you'd like to take a nap."

I said I might do that, after I'd unpacked, and she gave me a smile and left. I started stowing my things away.

I was pretty well satisfied with the way things were going. For a minute or two, I'd thought I was moving too fast, but it seemed to have worked out okay. With a dame like her, if she really liked you, you could practically throw away the brakes.

I finished unpacking, and stretched out on the bed with a true-detective story magazine.

I turned through the pages, locating the place I'd left off:

* * *

…thus the story of Charlie (Little) Bigger, the deadliest, most elusive killer in criminal history. The total number of his slayings-for-hire will probably never be known, but he has been officially charged with sixteen. He is wanted for murder in New York, Philadelphia, Chicago and Detroit.

Little Bigger vanished as from the face of the earth in 1943, immediately following the gangland slaying of his brother and contact-man, "Big Luke" Bigger. Exactly what became of him is still a topic for heated discussion in police and underworld circles. According to some rumors, he died years ago of tuberculosis. Others would have it that he was a victim of a revenge murder, like his brother, "Big." Still others maintain that he is alive. The truth, of course, is simply this: No one knows what happened to Little Bigger, because no one knew him. No one, that is, who survived the acquaintance.

All his contacts were made through his brother. He was never arrested, never fingerprinted, never photographed. No man, naturally, who was as murderously active as he could remain completely anonymous, and Little Bigger did not. But the picture we get, pieced from various sources, is more tantalizing than satisfying.

Assuming that he is still alive and unchanged, Little Bigger is a mild-looking little man, slightly over five feet tall and weighing approximately one hundred pounds. His eyes are weak, and he wears thick-lensed glasses. He is believed to be suffering from tuberculosis. His teeth are in very bad condition, and many of them are missing. He is quick-tempered, studious, a moderate smoker and drinker. He looks younger than the thirty to thirty-five years which, according to estimates, he is now.

Despite his appearance, Little bigger can be very ingratiating, particularly in the case of women…

I tossed the magazine aside. I sat up and kicked off the elevator shoes. I walked to the high-topped dresser, tilted the mirror down and opened my mouth. I took out my upper and lower plate. I pulled my eyelids back — first one, then the other — and removed the contact lenses.

I stood looking at myself a moment, liking the tan, liking the weight I'd put on. I coughed and looked into my handkerchief, and I didn't like that much.

I lay back down on the bed, thinking I was sure going to have to watch my health, wondering if it would do me much damage when I started making love to her.

I closed my eyes, thinking…about her…and him…and The Man…and Fruit Jar…and this crappy-puke looking house and the bare front yard and the squeaking steps and — and that gate.

My eyes snapped opened, then drooped shut again. I'd have to do something about that gate. Someone was liable to walk by the place and snag their clothes on it.

3

I met Mr. Kendall, the other boarder, on the way down to dinner. He was a dignified, little old guy—the kind who'd remain dignified if he got locked in a nickel toilet and had to crawl under the door. He said he was very happy to meet me, and that he would consider it a privilege to help me get settled in Peardale. I said that was nice of him.

"I was thinking about work," he said, as we went into the dining room. "Coming in late this way, it may be a little difficult. The part-time jobs are pretty well sewed up, by now. But I'll keep my eyes open at the bakery—we employ more student help than any place in town, I believe—and it's just possible that something can be worked out."

"I wouldn't want you to go to any trouble," I said.

"No trouble. After all, we're all living here together, and—ah, that looks very good, Mrs. Winroy."

"Thanks." She made a little face, brushing a wisp of hair out of her eyes. "We may as well see how it tastes. Heaven only knows when Jake will get here."

We all sat down. Mr. Kendall more or less took over the job of passing things, while she slumped in her chair, fanning her face with her hand. She hadn't been just kidding about throwing dinner together. Apparently she'd dashed out to the store for an armload of canned goods.

It wasn't bad, you understand. She'd bought a lot of everything, and it was all topgrade. But she could have done twice as well with half the money and a little more effort.

Mr. Kendall sampled his asparagus and said it was very good. He sampled the anchovies, the imported sardines and the potted tongue and said they were very good. He tapped his mouth with his napkin, and I was expecting him to say that *it* was very good. Or maybe he'd give her a nice juicy compliment on her can opener. Instead he turned and glanced toward the door, his head cocked a little to one side.

"That must be Ruth," he said, after a moment. "Don't you think so, Mrs. Winroy?"

Mrs. Winroy listened. She nodded. "Thank God," she sighed, and began to brighten up. "I was afraid she might stay away another day."

"Ruth is the young lady who works here," Mr. Kendall told me. "She's a student at the college, too. A very fine young woman, very deserving."

"Yeah?" I said. "Maybe I shouldn't say so, but it sounds to me like she's got a broken piston."

He gave me a blank look. Mrs. Winroy let out with the guffaw again.

"Silly!" she said. "That's her father's car, her Pa, she calls him. He drives her back and forth from their farm whenever she goes home for a visit."

There was a slight mimicking note to her voice, a tone that wasn't so much nasty as amused and contemptuous.

The car stopped in front of the house. A door opened and closed—slammed—and someone said, *"Now, you take keer o' yerself, Ruthie,"* and that broken piston began to clatter, and the car pulled away.

The gate squeaked. There was a footstep on the walk; just one footstep, and a tap; a kind of thud-tap. It—She—came up the walk, stepping and thud-tapping. She came up the steps— *thud-tap, thud-tap*—and across the porch.

Mr. Kendall shook his head at me sadly. "Poor girl," he said, dropping his voice.

Mrs. Winroy excused herself and got up.

She met Ruth at the front door and hustled her right down the hall and into the kitchen. So I didn't get a good look at her; rather, I should say, one good look was all I did get. But what I saw interested me. Maybe it wouldn't interest you, but it did me.

She had on an old mucklededung-colored coat—the way it was screaming Sears-Roebuck they should have paid her to wear it—and a kind of rough wool skirt. Her glasses were the kind your grandpa maybe wore, little tiny lenses, steel rims, pinchy across the nose. They made her eyes look like walnuts in a plate of cream fudge. Her hair was black and thick and shiny, but the way it was fixed—murder!

She only had one leg, the right one. The fingers of her left hand, gripping the crosspiece of her crutch, looked a little splayed.

I heard Mrs. Winroy ordering her around in the kitchen, not mean but pretty firm and fussy. I heard water running into the sink and pans clattering, and the *thud-tap, thud-tap, thud-tap,* moving faster and faster — humble, apologetic, anxious. I could almost hear her heart pounding with it.

Mr. Kendall passed me the sugar, then spooned some into his own coffee. "Tsk, tsk," he said. I'd been hearing people say that in books for years, but he was the first real-life guy I'd ever heard say it. "Such a sad thing for a fine young woman."

"Yeah," I said, "isn't it?"

"And there's nothing to be done about it, apparently. She'll have to go through life that way."

"You mean she can't raise the dough for an artificial leg?" I said. "There's ways of getting around that."

"We-el" — he looked down at his plate uncomfortably — "of course, the family *is* impoverished. But it's — well, it's not a question of money."

"What is it a question of?"

"Well — er — uh" — he was actually blushing — "I have no — uh — personal knowledge of the — er — situation, but I understand it's a — It's due to a very — uh — peculiar malformation of the — er —"

"Yeah?" I encouraged him.

"— of the left limb!" he finished.

He came out with it like it was a dirty word. I grinned to myself, and said "Yeah?" again. But he wasn't talking any more about Ruth's—uh—er—limb, and I didn't press him any. It made it more interesting not to know.

I could look forward to finding out about it myself.

He stuffed his pipe and lit up. He asked me if I'd ever noticed how so many deserving people—people who did their best to be decent—got so little out of life.

"Yes," I said.

"Well," he said, "I suppose every picture has its bright side. Ruthie couldn't get employment in any other household, and Mrs. Winroy couldn't—uh—Mrs. Winroy was having some difficulty in finding anyone. So it all works out nicely. Mrs. Winroy has a grateful and industrious servant. Ruth has her board and room and spending money. Five dollars a week now, I believe."

"No kidding!" I said. "Five dollars a week! That must put an awful strain on Mrs. Winroy."

"I suppose it does," he nodded seriously, "things being as they are. But Ruth's an unusually good worker."

"I should think she would be for that kind of money."

He took his pipe out of his mouth, and looked into the bowl. He glanced up at me, and he chuckled.

"I'm not much of a man to recite personal history, Mr. Bigelow, but—well, I was a teacher for a great many years. English literature. Yes, I taught here at the college for a time. My parents were living then, and I couldn't stretch my salary over the needs of the three of us; so I entered and remained in a more remunerative trade. But I've never lost my interest in literature, particularly in the satirists—"

"I see," I said, and it was my turn to blush a little.

"It's always seemed to me that satire cannot exist outside the rarefied atmosphere of excellence. It is either excellent or it is nothing...I should be very glad to lend you my *Gulliver's Travels*, Mr. Bigelow. Also the collected works of Lucilius, Juvenal, Butler—"

"That's enough. That's more than enough." I held up a hand, grinning. "I'm sorry, Mr. Kendall."

"Quite all right," he nodded placidly. "You had no way of knowing, of course, but a student who earns five dollars a week and her board and room in a college town—*this* town, at least—is doing very well for herself."

"Sure," I said. "I don't doubt it a bit."

All at once I'd had a crazy idea about him, one that kind of gave me the whimwhams. Because maybe everyone doesn't have a price, but if this dull, dignified old guy *did* have one...Well, he'd be worth almost anything he asked as an ace in the hole. He could throw in with me, in case of a showdown: back me up in a story, or actually give me a hand if there was no other way out. Otherwise, he'd just keep tabs on me, see that I didn't try a runout...

But that was crazy. I've already said so. The Man knew I couldn't run. He knew I wouldn't fluff the job. I shoved the idea out of my mind, shoved it damned good and hard. You just can't play around with notions like that.

Mrs. Winroy came in from the kitchen, picking up her purse from the sideboard. She paused at the table.

"I don't want to rush you gentlemen, but I think Ruth would like to clear up here whenever you're through."

"Certainly, certainly." Mr. Kendall pushed back his chair. "Shall we take our coffee into the living room, Mr. Bigelow?"

"Why don't you take Carl's cup for him?" she said. "I'd like to speak to him for a moment."

"Certainly. Of course," he said.

He took our cups and crossed the hall into the living room. I followed her out onto the porch.

It was dark out there. She stood up close to me. "You stinker," she said accusingly, half laughing. "I heard you giving him the rib...So I'm putting a strain on myself, am I?"

"Hell," I said, "you couldn't expect me to pass up an opening like that. As a matter of fact, when it comes to an attractive opening I —"

She snickered. "But look, Carl — honey..."

"Yeah?" I said. I brought my hands up to her hips.

"I've got to run downtown for a while, honey. I'll get back as soon as I can, but if Jake shows up while I'm gone, don't — well, don't pay any attention to him."

"That could be quite a job," I said.

"I mean he's almost sure to be drunk. He always is when he's late this way. But it's all talk with him; he hasn't got any real guts. Just don't pay any attention to anything he says, and everything will be all right."

I said I'd do my best. There was nothing else I could say. She gave me a quick hard kiss. Then she wiped my mouth with her handkerchief and started down the steps.

"Remember, Carl. Just don't pay attention to him."

"I'll remember," I said.

Mr. Kendall was waiting, worriedly, afraid that my coffee would be cold. I said it was fine, just the way I liked it, and he leaned back and relaxed. He started talking about finding a job for me—he'd taken it for granted that I'd need one. He moved from the subject of a job for me to that of his own job. As I got it, he was the manager of the place, the kind of manager who doesn't have the title and who works all hours for a few bucks more than the regular hired hands get.

I believe he was all set to take the night off by way of giving me a full and complete history of the baking industry. As it worked out, though, he hadn't been spouting for more than ten or fifteen minutes when Jake Winroy arrived.

You've seen pictures of Jake, of course; anyone who reads the newspapers has. But the pictures you've seen were probably taken when he was still in there punching. For the Jake you've seen and the one I saw were two different people.

He was a tall guy, around six feet, I guess, and his normal weight was around two hundred pounds. But he couldn't have weighed more than a hundred and forty now. The skin on his face hung in folds. It seemed to tug at his mouth, drawing it downward; it tugged down at the pouches of his eyes. Even his nose dropped. It sagged out of his face like a melting candle in a pan of dirty tallow. He was stooped, curve-shouldered. His chin almost touched his neck, and his neck seemed to bend and wobble from the weight of his head.

He was very drunk, of course. He had every right to be. Because he was dead, the same as; and I guess he knew it.

He got snagged coming through the gate—I'd known

damned well that gate would snag someone—and when he
yanked himself free he went sprawling and stumbling almost to
the porch. He got up the steps, falling back two for every one he
took, it sounded like. He came across the porch in a kind of
staggering rush. He staggered into the hall. He stood weaving
and swaying there a moment, blinking his eyes and trying to get
his bearings.

"Mr. Winroy!" Mr. Kendall edged toward him nervously.
"Would you—uh—may I help you to bed, Mr. Winroy?"

"B-bed?" Jake hiccuped. "W-hhh-hoo y-you?"

"Now, you know very well who I am, sir!"

"S-sure. I k-now, but duh-duh duh d-you? Betcha c-can' tell
me, can you?"

Mr. Kendall's mouth tightened. "Would you like to come
over to the bakery with me for a while, Mr. Bigelow?"

"I think I'll go up to my room," I said. "I—"

And Jake jumped like he'd been shot.

He jumped and whirled at the sound of my voice. He looked
at me, wild-eyed, and one of his long, veined hands came up,
pointing. "W-who y-you?"

"This is Mr. Bigelow," said Mr. Kendall. "Your new boarder."

"Oh, yeah? Yeah!" He took a step backward, keeping his eyes
fixed on me. "B-boarder, huh? So h-he-s the new b-boarder,
huh? Oh, y-yeah?"

"Of course, he's the new boarder!" Kendall snapped. "A very
fine young man, and you're certainly doing your best to make
him uncomfortable! Now, why—"

"Oh, yuh-yeah? Yeah!" He kept on edging toward the door,

edging backward in a sort of half crouch. His eyes peered out at me wildly through the tumbled strands of his greasy black hair. "N-new b-boarder. Makin' h-huh-him uncomfortable. *Huh-him* uncomfortable! Oh, y-yeah?"

It was like a broken record — a broken record with a rasping, worn-out needle. He made me think of some wild sick animal, trapped in a corner.

"Oh, y-yeah? Yeah!" He didn't seem to be able to stop it. All he could do was back up, back, back, back...

"This is disgusting, sir! You know quite well you've been expecting Mr. Bigelow. I was present when you talked about it with Mrs. Winroy."

"Oh, y-yeah? Yeah! 'S-spectin' Mr. Bigelow, yeah? 'S-spectin' Mr. B-Bigger-low..."

His back touched against the screen door.

And he tripped on the lintel, plunged stumbling across the porch and went crashing down the steps. He turned a complete somersault on the way down.

"Oh, my goodness!" Mr. Kendall snapped on the porch light. "*Oh,* my goodness! He's probably killed himself!"

Wringing his hands, he scuttled across the porch and started down the steps. And I sauntered after him. But Jake Winroy wasn't dead, and he didn't want any help from me.

"Nnnnuh-NO!" he yelled. "N-NUHNUH—NO!..."

He rolled to his feet. He sprang awkwardly toward the gate, and he tripped and went down again. He picked himself up and shot staggering into the road.

He took off right down the middle of it toward town. Arms

flapping, legs weaving and wobbling crazily. Running, because there was nothing to do but run.

I felt pretty sorry for him. He didn't need to let his house look like it did, and I couldn't excuse him for it. But I still felt sorry.

"Please don't let this upset you, Mr. Bigelow." Kendall touched my arm. "He simply goes a little crazy when he gets too much liquor in him."

"Sure," I said. "I understand. My father was a pretty heavy drinker... Let's get the light off, huh?"

I jerked my head over my shoulder. A bunch a yokels had come out of the bar and were staring across the street at us.

I turned the light off, and we stood on the porch talking a few minutes. He said he hoped Ruthie hadn't been alarmed. He invited me to the bakery again, and I turned him down.

He stuffed tobacco into his pipe, puffed at it nervously. "I can't tell you how much I admired your self-possession, Mr. Bigelow. I'm afraid I—I've always thought I was pretty cool and collected, but—"

"You are," I said. "You were swell. It's just that you're not used to drunks."

"You say your—uh—your father—?"

It was strange that I'd mentioned it. I mean, there wasn't any harm in mentioning it; but it had been so long ago, more than thirty years ago.

"Of course, I don't remember anything about it," I said. "That was back in 1930 and I was only a baby at the time; but my mother—" That was one lie I had to pound home. My age.

"Tsk, tsk! Poor woman. How terrible for her!"

"He was a coal miner," I said. "Over around McAlester, Oklahoma. The union didn't amount to much in those days, and I don't need to tell you there was a depression. About the only work a man could get was in the wildcats, working without inspection. Stripping pillars—"

I paused a moment, remembering. Remembering the stooped back, and the glaring fear-maddened eyes. Remembering the choked sounds at night, the sobbing screams.

"He got the idea that we were trying to kill him," I said. "If we spilled a little meal, or tore our clothes or something like that, he'd beat the tar out of us...Out of the others, I mean. I was only a baby."

"Yes? But I don't understand why—"

"It's simple," I said. "Anyway, it was simple enough to him. It seemed to him that we were trying to keep him in the mines. Keeping him from getting away. Using up stuff as fast as we could so that he'd have to stay down there under the ground... until he was buried under it."

Mr. Kendall tsk-tsk'ed again. "Wretched! Poor deluded fellow. As if you could help—"

"We couldn't help it," I nodded, "but that didn't make it any better for him. He had to work in the mines, and when a man has to do something he does it. But that doesn't make it any easier. You might even say it was twice as hard that way. You're not brave or noble or unselfish or any of the things a man likes to think he is. You're just a cornered rat, and you start acting like one."

"Mmm. You seem to be an unusually introspective young man, Mr. Bigelow. You say your father died of drink?"

"No," I said. "He died in the mines. There was so much rock on top of him that it took a week to dig him out."

Mr. Kendall shoved off for the bakery after a few more tsks and how-terribles, and I went back in the house. Then I sauntered on back to the kitchen.

She was bent over the sink, the crutch gripped under her armpit, washing what looked like about a thousand dishes. Apparently, Mrs. Winroy had saved them up for her while she'd been away—them and every other dirty job.

I hung my coat over a chair and rolled up my sleeves. I picked up a big spoon and began scraping the pans out.

I got them all scraped into one pan, and started for the back door with it.

She hadn't looked at me since I'd come into the room, and she didn't look at me now. But she did manage to speak. The words came out in a rush like a kid who's nerved to recite a poem and has to do it fast or not at all.

"The g-garbage can's at the side of the porch—"

"You mean they don't have any chickens?" I said. "Why, they ought to have some chickens to feed it to."

"Y-yes," she said.

"It's a shame to waste food this way. With all the hungry people there are in the world."

"I—I think so, too," she said, sort of breathless.

That was all she was up to for the moment. She was blushing like a house afire, and her head was ducked so far over the sink I was afraid she would fall in. I took the garbage outside and scraped it out slowly.

I knew how she felt. Why wouldn't I know how it felt to be a kind of joke, to have people tell you off kind of like it was what you were made for? You never get used to it, but you get to where you don't expect anything else.

She was still pretty shocked by the idea of having talked to me when I went back inside. But being shocked didn't keep her from liking it. She said I s-shouldn't be helping her wipe the dishes—then, pointed out a towel to me. She said h-hadn't I better put an apron on; she did it for me, her fingers trembling but lingering.

We stood wiping the dishes together, our arms touching now and then. The first few times it happened, she jerked hers away like she'd brushed against a hot stove. Then, pretty soon, she wasn't jerking away. And, once, when my elbow brushed her breast, it seemed to me that she sort of leaned into it.

Studying her out of the corner of my eyes, I saw that I'd been right about her left hand. The fingers *were* splayed. She didn't have the full use of it, and she kept trying to hide it from me. Even with that, though, and her leg—whatever was wrong with her leg—she had plenty on the ball.

All that hard work and deep breathing had put breasts on her like daddy-come-to-church. And swinging around on that crutch hadn't done her rear end any harm. If you saw it by itself, you might have thought it belonged to a Shetland pony. But I don't mean it was big. It was the way it was put on her: the way it hinged into the flat stomach and the narrow waist. It was as though she'd been given a break there for all the places she'd been shortchanged.

I got her to talking. I got her to laughing. I draped another dishtowel over my head and started prancing around; and she leaned back against the drainboard, giggling and blushing and protesting.

"S-stop, now, Carl—" Her eyes were shining. The sun had come up behind them, and was shining out at me. "Y-you stop, now—"

"Stop what?" I said, pouring it on all the harder. "What do you want me to stop, Ruth? You mean *this* or *this?*"

I kept it up, sizing her up while I did it, and I changed my mind about a couple of things. I decided I wasn't going to give her any tips on dressing. I wasn't going to fix her up with a compact and a permanent. Because any dolling up she did need, she'd do for herself, and she didn't really need any.

Then, suddenly, she wasn't laughing any more. She stopped and stood staring over my shoulder.

I knew what it must be. I'd had a hunch it was coming. I turned slowly around, and I was damned careful to keep my hands away from my sides.

I can't say whether he'd rung the doorbell and we hadn't heard him, or whether he'd just walked in without ringing. But there he was—a tall rawboned guy with sharp but friendly blue eyes, and a graying coffee-stained mustache.

"Havin' quite a time for yourself, hey, kids?" he said. "Well, that's fine. Nothing I like better'n to see young folks enjoying themselves."

Ruth's mouth opened and closed. I waited, smiling.

"Been meaning to get out and see your folks, Miss Dorne," he went on. "Hear you got a new baby out there... Don't believe I've ever met you, young fellow. I'm Bill Summers—Sheriff Summers."

"How do you do, sheriff," I said, and I shook hands with him. "I'm Carl Bigelow."

"Hope I didn't startle you folks just now. Dropped over to see a fellow named—*Bigelow!* You say *you're* Carl Bigelow?"

"Yes, sir," I said. "Is there something wrong, sheriff?"

He looked me over slowly, frowning, taking in the apron and the dishtowel on my head; looking like he couldn't decide whether to laugh or start cussing.

"I reckon we've got some talking to do, Bigelow... Darn that Jake Winroy's hide, anyway!"

4

We were in my room. Mrs. Winroy had come in a couple of minutes behind him, and she'd blown her lid so high we'd had to come upstairs.

"I just can't understand it," I said. "Mr. Winroy's known I was coming for several weeks. If he didn't want me here, why in the world didn't—"

"Well, o'course, he hadn't seen you then. What with seein' you and connecting you up with a name that sounds kinda like yours—well, I can see where it might give him a little start. A man that's in the fix Jake Winroy's in."

"If anyone's got a right to feel upset, it's me. I can tell you this, sheriff. If I'd known that James C. Winroy was Jake Winroy, I wouldn't be here now."

"Uh-huh, sure." He shook his head sympathetically. "But I was kind of wonderin' about that, son. Why did you come here, anyway? All the way from Arizona to a place like Peardale."

"That was it partly," I shrugged. "Because it was a long way from Arizona. As long as I was making a fresh start, I thought I'd better make a clean break of it. It's not easy to make

something out of yourself around people who remember you
when you weren't anything."

"Uh-huh. Yeah?"

"That was only part of it, of course," I said. "This was cheap,
and the school would accept me as a special student. There aren't
many colleges that will, you know. If you don't have a high-
school education, you're out of luck." I laughed shortly, making
it sound pretty grim and dispirited. "It seems pretty crazy to
me, now. I'd dreamed about it for years — getting myself a little
education and landing a good job and — and — But I guess I
should have known better."

"Aw, now, son" — he cleared his throat, looking troubled —
"don't take it that way. I know there ain't no sense to this, and I
don't like it a bit better than you do. But I ain't got no choice,
Jake Winroy being what he is. Now you just help me out and
we'll get this settled in no time."

"I'll tell you anything I can, Sheriff Summers," I said.

"Swell. What about kinfolks?"

"My father's dead. My mother and the rest of the family — I
don't know about them. We started splitting up right after Dad
died. It's been so long ago that I've even forgotten what they
looked like."

"Uh-huh?" he said. "Yeah?"

I started talking. Nothing I told him could be checked, but I
could see he believed me; and it would have been strange if he
hadn't. The story was pretty much true, you see. It was practically
gospel, except for the dates. There was a hell of a depression in
the Oklahoma coal fields in the early twenties. There were strikes

and the militia was called in, and no one had money enough for grub, let alone doctors and undertakers. And there was plenty to think about besides birth and death certificates.

I told him how we'd drifted over into Arkansas, picking cotton, and then on down into the Rio Grande Valley for the fruit, and then over into the Imperial for the stoop crops… Sticking together, at first, then splitting up for a day or two at a time to follow the work. Splitting up and staying split up.

I'd sold newspapers in Houston. I'd caddied in Dallas. I'd hustled programs and pop in Kansas City. And in Denver, in front of the Brown Palace Hotel, I'd put the bite on a big flashy-looking guy for coffee money. And he'd said, "Jesus, Charlie, you don't remember me? I'm your brother, Luke—"

But I left that part out, of course.

"Uh-huh"—he cut in on me. I'd given him so much he was getting tired. "When did you go to Arizona?"

"December of '44. I've never been real sure of my birthdate, but I'd just turned sixteen as near as I can figure it. Anyway"—I made a point of being careful about it—"I don't see how I could have been more than seventeen."

"Sure," he nodded, scowling a little. "Anyone'd know that. Don't see how you could even have been sixteen."

"Well, the war was still on and any kind of help was hard to get. This Mr. Fields and his wife—awfully nice old couple—gave me a job in their filling station, and it didn't pay much, because it didn't make much, but I liked it fine. I lived with them, just like I was their son, and saved everything I did make. And two years ago, when Da—I mean, Mr. Fields died, I bought the place from her...I guess"—I hesitated—"I guess that's one reason I wanted to get away from Tucson. With Dad Fields dead and Mom moved back to Iowa, it just didn't seem like home any more."

The sheriff coughed and blew his nose. "Dang that Jake," he growled. "So you sold out and came back here, eh?"

"Yes, sir," I said. "Would you like to see a copy of the bill of sale?"

I showed it to him. I also showed him some of the letters Mrs. Fields had written me from Iowa before she died. He paid a lot more attention to them than he had to the bill of sale, and when he was through he blew his nose again.

"Goldarn it, Carl, I'm really sorry to've put you through all this, but I reckon I'm not through yet. You won't mind if I do a little telegraphin' out there to Tucson? I just about got to, you know. Otherwise Jake'll keep kickin' up a fuss like a chicken with its head off."

"You mean"—I paused—"you want to get in touch with the chief of police in Tucson?"

"You ain't got no objections, have you?"

"No," I said. "I just never got to know him as well as I did some of the other folks. Could you send a wire to the sheriff, too, and County Judge McCafferty? I used to take care of their cars for them."

"Goldang it!" he said, and got to his feet.

I stood up also. "Will this take very long, sheriff? I hardly feel like enrolling at the college until it's settled."

"O'course, you don't," he nodded sympathetically. "We'll have it all straightened out, so's you can start in next Monday."

"I'd have liked to get into New York first," I said. "I won't go, naturally, until you say it's all right. But I bought a new suit while I was there, and the alterations were supposed to be done by this Saturday."

I walked to the bedroom door with him, and it seemed to me I heard a faint creak from the door across the hall.

"A man's kinda got to get along with everyone in a job like mine, so I wouldn't want you to repeat anything. But these Winroys—well, it ain't good economy to stay with 'em, no matter how cheap it is. You take my advice, an'—"

"Yes?" I said.

"No"—he sighed, and shook his head—"I guess you can't very well do that. Jake kicks up a big fuss, and then you move out, an' no matter what I say or you say it looks bad. Makes it look like you had to move, like maybe there was somethin' to his crazy carryin' on."

"Yes, sir," I said. "I surely wish I'd known who he was before I came here."

I saw him out the door, and closed it again. I stretched out on the bed with a cigarette, lay with my eyes half closed, puffing smoke at the ceiling. I felt all wrung out. No matter how well prepared you are for a deal like that, it takes a lot out of you. I wanted to rest, to be left alone for a while. And the door opened and Mrs. Winroy came in.

"Carl," she said huskily, sitting down on the edge of the bed. "I'm so sorry, darling. I'll murder that Jake when I get my hands on him!"

"Forget it," I said. "Where is he, anyway?"

"At his shop, probably. Probably'll spend the night there. He'd better if he knows what's good for him!"

I walked my fingers up her thigh, and let them do a little wandering around. After a moment or two, she squeezed them absently and laid my hand back on the bed.

"Carl... You're not angry?"

"I didn't like it," I said, "but I'm not angry. Matter of fact, I feel pretty sorry for Jake."

"He's losing his marbles. Why, they wouldn't dare kill him! It would hurt them twice as much as having him testify."

"Yeah?" I said. "I guess I don't know much about those things, Mrs. Winroy."

"They—Why don't you call me Fay, honey? When we're alone like this."

"Fay honey," I said.

"They wouldn't dare to, would they, Carl? Right here in his home town where everyone knows him and he knows everyone? Why—why"—she laughed irritably—"my God! this is the one place in the world where he's safe. No stranger can get near him—no one he doesn't know, and—"

"I got near him," I said.

"Oh, well," she shrugged. "I'm not counting you. He knows that anyone the college sent here would be all right."

"Yeah? He didn't act much like it."

"Because he's full of booze! He's beginning to see things!"

"Well," I said, "whatever he does, you can't blame him much."

"I can't, huh?"

"I don't think you should," I said.

43

I raised up on one elbow and tamped out my cigarette.

"Here's the way I might look at it, Fay," I said, "if I were in Jake's shoes. Practically all I know about crime is what I read in the papers. But I'm pretty good at putting myself in the other fellow's place, and here's the way I'd feel if I were Jake. I'd figure that if they took a notion to kill me, there wouldn't be any way I could stop them. Nothing I could do, no place I could go. I—"

"But, Carl—"

"If they didn't get me in one place, they'd do it in another. Some place, somehow, and no matter how tough it was. I'd know they'd get me, Fay."

"But they won't! They can't afford to!"

"Sure," I said.

"The case won't ever come to trial. Everyone says it won't!"

"Well, they probably know," I said. "I was just talking about how Jake would feel if he thought they *did* want to kill him."

"Yes, but you said—I mean, when he knows they won't do it, why—?"

"He knows it, but do they know it? See what I mean? He knows they've got plenty of brains and plenty of money. He knows they'd find an angle, if they wanted to get him badly enough."

"But they—"

"They don't," I said. "But if they did? There wouldn't be anyone Jake could trust. Why, they might even try to get to him through old man Kendall."

"Oh, Carl! That's ridiculous!"

"Sure, it is," I said, "but you get the idea. Some guy who would never be suspected."

"Carl—"

She was looking narrow-eyed, interested, cautious.

"Yeah, Fay?" I said.

"You... What if—if—"

"What if what?" I said.

She kept on staring at me in that puzzled cautious way. Then, she laughed suddenly and jumped up. "God," she said. "Talk about Jake losing *his* marbles! Look, Carl. You're not going to school this week?"

I shook my head. I didn't bother to rib her about snooping.

"Well, Ruth has a nine o'clock class, so you ought to be downstairs by eight if you want her to fix your breakfast. Or you can just help yourself to coffee and toast or something whenever you get up. That's what I usually do."

"Thanks," I said. "I'll see how I feel in the morning."

She left, then. I opened a window and stretched back out on the bed. I needed a bath, but I wasn't up to it yet. I wasn't up to such a little thing as undressing and walking a few steps down the hall to the bathroom.

I lay still, forcing myself to lie still when I felt the urge to get up and look in the mirror. You've got to take it easy. You can't run for the big score with sand in your shoes. I closed my eyes, looking at myself in my mind's eye.

It gave me a start. It was like looking at someone else.

I'd seen myself that way ten thousand times and each time it was a new experience. I'd see what other people seemed to see, and I'd catch myself thinking, "Gosh, what a nice little guy. You don't need anyone to tell you *he's* all right—"

I thought that, now, and somehow it sent a shiver through me. I started thinking about the teeth and the other chances, and I knew that they really didn't matter. But I made myself think about them.

I felt safer, some way, believing it was those things instead of—instead of?

...The teeth and the contact lenses. The tanned, healthy-looking face. The extra weight. The added height...and only part of it was due to the elevator shoes I'd worn since 1943. I'd straightened up when I shook the bug, and—but had I shaken it? Suppose I took sick now, so sick I couldn't go through with this? The Man would be sore, and—the name? *Charles Bigger*—Carl Bigelow? Well, it was as good as any. It wouldn't have been any better to call myself Chester Bellows or Chauncey Billingsley; and it would have had to be something like that. A man can't get too far away from his own name, you know. He may try to but he's asking for trouble. There's laundry markings. There's answering when you're spoken to. So...

So I hadn't made any mistakes. I...But The Man had found me. He'd never seen me before either but he'd known right where to send for me. And if The Man could do it...

I lighted a cigarette, jabbed it out immediately, and threw myself back on the pillows.

The Man—you couldn't count The Man. I hadn't made any mistakes, and I wouldn't make any. I'd make the score, and I'd make the afterwards, the hard part. Because no matter how smoothly it was done, there was bound to be some heat. And the surest way of getting cooked was to try to run from it.

You'd screw things up for The Man. If they didn't get you, he would.

So...I felt drowsy.

No mistakes. No letting down for even a second. No getting sick. And use them all, Mrs. Winroy directly, the others indirectly. They'd have to be on my side. They'd have to *know* that I couldn't do what I had to do. The Man didn't need to watch me. They would. They were all watching to see that I did it right, and...watching...always watching...and me...

...They crowded the sidewalks of that dark narrow street, that narrow and lonely street. And they were going on about their business, laughing and talking and enjoying life; but still they were watching me. Watching me follow Jake and watching The Man follow me. I was sweating and all out of breath, because I'd been in the street a long time. And they kept getting in my way, getting between me and Jake, but they never got in The Man's way. Me, ME, they had to screw up. And...I could taste the black damp in my mouth and I could hear the pillars cracking and crumbling and the lamp on my cap began to flicker and...I grabbed one of the bastards. I grabbed himher, and yanked and rolled and...

I had her on the bed. She was under me, and I had the crutch across her throat, pinned down with my arms.

I blinked, staring down at her, fighting to come out of the dream. I said, "Jesus, kid. You don't want to ever —"

I slid the crutch to one side and she started breathing again, but she still couldn't talk. She was too scared. I looked into the great scared eyes — *watching me* — and it was all I could do to keep from slugging her.

"Spill it," I said. "Spit it out. What were you doing here?"

"I—I—I—"

I dug my hand into her side, and twisted. And she gasped.

"Spill it."

"I—I—I w-was a-afraid for you. I—I w-was w-worried about... *Carl!* D-don't—"

She began to struggle, then, and I lay flat against her. I held her, twisting her, and she gasped and moaned. She tried to pull at my hand, and I twisted harder.

"D-don't!...I've n-never...C-carl, I've never...it's n-not n-n-nice and *Carl! Carl!* Y-you've g-got to...I'll have a b-baby, and—"

...She'd stopped begging.

There was nothing left to beg for.

I looked down, my head against hers so that she couldn't see that I was looking. I looked, and I closed my eyes quickly. But I couldn't keep them closed.

It was a baby's foot. A tiny little foot and ankle. It started just above the knee joint—where the knee would have been if she had one—a tiny little ankle, not much bigger around than a thumb; a baby ankle and a baby foot.

The toes were curling and uncurling, moving with the rhythm of her body...

"C-Carl...Oh, *C-Carl!*" she gasped.

After a long time, what seemed like a long time, I heard her saying, "Don't. Please don't, Carl. It's a-all right, so—so, please, Carl...Please don't cry any more—"

5

I was a long time getting to sleep, and thirty minutes after I did I woke up again. I woke up exhausted, but with the feeling that I'd been asleep for hours. You know? It went on like that all night.

When I woke the last time it was nine-thirty, and sunlight was streaming into the room. It was shining right on my pillows, and my face felt hot and moist. I sat up quickly, hugging my stomach. The light, hitting into my eyes suddenly, had made me sick. I clenched my eyes against it, but the light wasn't shut out. It seemed to be closed in, under the lids, and a thousand little images danced in its brilliance. Tiny white things, little figure-seven-shaped things: dancing and twisting and squirming.

I sat on the edge of the bed, rocking and hugging myself. I could taste the blood in my mouth, salty and sour, and I thought of how it would look in the sunlight, how yellow and purplish, and...

Somehow I got to the dresser and got the lenses and teeth into place. I staggered down the hall, kicked the bathroom door shut behind me, and went down on my knees in front of the

49

toilet bowl. I threw my arms around it, bracing myself, looking down at the wavering water in the faintly brown-stained porcelain. And then my whole body swelled and shook, and I heaved.

The first one, the first heave, was the worst. It seemed to pull me two ways, forcing the stuff back and throwing it up at the same time. After that it was easier; the hard part was getting my breath, keeping from strangling. My heart pounded harder and harder. The sweat of weakness streamed down off my face, mixing with the blood and the vomit. I knew I was making a hell of a racket, but I didn't care.

There was a rap on the door, and Fay Winroy called, "Carl. Are you all right, Carl?" I didn't answer. I couldn't. And the door opened.

"Carl! What in the world, honey—?"

I gestured with one hand, not looking around. Gestured that I was all right, that I was sorry, to get the hell out.

She said, "I'll be right back, honey," and I heard her hurrying back up the hall and down the stairs.

I flushed the toilet, keeping my eyes closed.

By the time she came back I'd got some cold water dabbed on my face and was sitting on the toilet seat. I was weak as all hell, but the sickness was gone.

"Drink it down, baby," she said. And I drank it down—a half a glass of straight whiskey. I gasped and shuddered, and she said, "Here. Take a deep drag." And I took the cigarette she handed me, and dragged on it deeply.

The whiskey stayed down, warming me and cooling me in all the places where I needed warming and cooling.

Savage Night

"My God, honey!..." She was down on her knees in front of me; why she bothered to wear that nightgown I didn't know, because it didn't conceal anything. "You get that way very much, Carl?"

I shook my head. "I haven't had a spell like that since I was a kid. Don't know what the hell brought it on."

"Well, gosh, I didn't know what to think. You sounded worse than Jake does sometimes."

She was smiling, concerned for me. But there was a calculating look in the reddish brown eyes. Was I a sharp guy, a guy who could give her a lot of kicks? Or was I just a sick punk, someone good for a lousy fifteen a week and no laughs to go with it?

Apparently she made up her mind. She stood up and locked her arms around mine, holding them. She said, "Mmmmmmmmph!" and kissed me open-mouthed. "You tough little bastard!" she whispered. "Oh, you tough little bastard! I've got half a notion to —"

I didn't want that. Yet. I wasn't up to it. So I started a little rough-house, and that broke the mood.

"Stinker!" she laughed, leaning against the wall of the hall-way. "Don't you dare, you naughty bad boy!"

"Flag me down, then," I said. "I only stop for red flags."

I looked at her standing there laughing, everything she had on view. And all the time telling me not to look, not to dare. I watched her, listened to her. I watched and listened to myself, standing outside myself. And it was like seeing a movie you've seen a thousand times before. And...and I guess there wasn't anything strange about that.

51

I shaved and took the bath I'd missed the night before. I got dressed, hurrying it up a little when she called up the stairs to me, and went down to the kitchen.

She'd fixed bacon and eggs and toast, some sliced oranges and french fries. And she'd dirtied up about half the pans and dishes in the place to do it, but it was all well prepared. She sat across from me at the kitchen table, kidding and laughing, keeping my coffee cup filled. And I knew what she was—but I couldn't help liking her.

We finished eating, and I passed her a cigarette.

"Carl—"

"Yes?" I said.

"About—about what we were talking about last night—"

She waited. I didn't say anything.

"Oh, hell," she said, finally. "Well, I suppose I'd better go downtown and see Jake. He can stay away as long as he wants to, but he's got to give me some money."

"Too bad you have to look him up," I said. "You don't think he'll be home?"

"Who knows what he'll do?" She shrugged angrily. "He'll probably stay away until they find out about you."

"I'm sorry," I said. "I hate to have him put himself out on my account."

She gave me another of those thoughtful looks, her eyes narrowed behind the smoke. "Carl. It will be all right, won't it? The sheriff—he—it'll be all right?"

"Why not?" I said.

"You're going to go to school here?"

"It would be pretty foolish not to," I said. "Wouldn't it?"

"Oh, I don't know. Skip it!" She laughed, irritably. "I guess I'm kind of goofy this morning."

"It's this town," I said. "Sticking around a hole like this with nothing to do. You just weren't built for it. You've got too much stuff for the place. I knew it the minute I saw you."

"Did you, honey?" She patted my hand.

"I should think you could get some kind of singing job," I said. "Something that would give you a better life."

"Yeah. Maybe. I don't know," she said. "If I had some clothes, the dough to look around with. Maybe I could, but I don't know, Carl. I've been out of things so long. I don't know whether I could work any more, even to get away from this."

I nodded. I took another step. It was probably unnecessary, but it wasn't any trouble and it could save a lot.

"You're afraid, too, aren't you," I said, "that things might be made a little unpleasant for Jake Winroy's wife?"

"Afraid?" She frowned, puzzledly. "Why should—?"

It had never occurred to her, apparently. And I could see it sink in on her now, sink and build and spread. It pushed the color out of her face, and her lips trembled.

"B-but it wasn't my fault. They can't blame me, Carl! H-how could they—they wouldn't blame me, would they, Carl?"

"They shouldn't," I said. "I don't suppose they would, if they knew how you felt."

"Carl! What can I—My God, honey, I don't know why I didn't see that—"

53

I laughed softly. It was time to call a halt. Her imagination could talk a lot better to her than I could. "Gosh," I said, "look at the time. Almost eleven o'clock, and we're still fooling around with breakfast."

"But, Carl. I—"

"Forget it." I grinned at her. "What would I know about things like that? Now you run on to town."

I stood up and began clearing away the dishes. After a long moment she got up, too, but she didn't make any move toward the door.

I took her by the shoulders and gave her a little shake. "It's like I said," I told her. "The town's getting on your nerves. You ought to run into the city for the weekend."

She smiled weakly, still pale around the gills. "Run is right. I sure as hell couldn't ride."

"Maybe you could," I said. "You got any kinfolks there? Anyone you ever visit?"

"Well, I have a sister over in the Bronx, but—"

"She'd yes for you? Give you an alibi in case Jake tried to check up?"

"Well, I don't—Why should I—?" She frowned at me, blinking; and I thought maybe I'd figured her wrong or had crowded her too hard. Then she laughed softly, huskily. "Boy!" she said. "Did I say he was slick? But look, Carl. Won't it look kind of funny if we both—?"

"We won't," I said. "You let me figure it out."

"All right, Carl." She nodded quickly. "You don't—you won't think I'm a tramp, will you? It's just that—"

"No," I said. "You're not a tramp."

"I'll go along as long as I can with a person, but when I'm through, well, I'm through. I just don't want any part of 'em any more. You understand Carl?"

"I understand," I said. "Now, beat it, will you? Or you stay here and I'll clear out. It doesn't look good for the two of us to be hanging around here alone."

"All right, honey. I'll go right now. And—oh, yes, don't bother about the dishes. Ruth can do them."

"Will you get out of here?" I said.

And she laughed and kissed me, and got out.

I cleared up the dishes and put them away. I uncovered an old rusty hammer and went out into the back yard. There was part of a packing crate lying against the alley fence. I knocked some nails out of it, walked around to the front, and went to work on that gate.

There hadn't been much of anything wrong with it in the beginning; a couple of nails in the hinges would have fixed it up fine. But just letting it go—trying to slam it when it couldn't slam had damned near wrecked it.

I was still hard at it when Kendall came home from the bakery to lunch.

"Ah," he said, approvingly, "I see you're like me, Mr. Bigelow. You like to keep busy."

"Yeah," I said. "It's something to pass the time."

"I heard about your—uh—little difficulty last night. I'm glad to see you're taking it in your stride. I—uh—don't want to seem presumptuous, but I've taken a strong personal interest

55

in you, Mr. Bigelow. I'd have been very disappointed if you'd allowed your plans to be upset by a drunken bum."

I said, yeah, or thanks, or something of the kind.

"Well," he said, "shall we go in? I think lunch must be ready."

I told him I'd just finished breakfast. "I guess you'll be the only one eating lunch, Mr. Kendall. Mrs. Winroy's gone to town, and I don't imagine Mr. Winroy will be here either."

"I'll tell Ruthie," he said, quickly. "The poor child's liable to go to a lot of trouble for nothing."

He went on inside, and I went back to work. After a moment he came out again.

"Uh, Mr. Bigelow," he called. "Do you know where Ruth might be?"

"I haven't seen anything of her," I said. "I didn't know whether she was supposed to come home at noon."

"Of course she is! Certainly." He sounded a little annoyed. "She gets out of her last morning class at eleven, and she's always here by eleven-thirty to start fixing lunch."

"Well," I said, and picked up my hammer again. He fidgeted on the porch uncertainly.

"I can't understand it," he frowned. "She's always here by eleven-thirty. She has to be to fix lunch and get the beds made before she goes back to school."

"Yeah," I said. "I can see how she would."

I finished working on the gate. I lit a cigarette, and sat down on the steps to rest.

Ruth. Ruthie. I'd dreaded facing her after last night. She'd asked for it, creeping in on me that way, and yeah, yeah, she'd wanted it, and she'd said it was all right. But someone defense-less, someone — a *baby*...

But now I wanted to see her. I wanted to see her more than anything in the world. It was like part of me was missing.

I puffed at the cigarette. I flipped it away, and lit up another one. I thought about her — me — swinging along on that crutch, head down, afraid to look at people, afraid to see them looking. You do all you can, and it's still not enough. You keep your head down, knocking yourself out. You take all the shortcuts...

I got up and started around the house. I almost ran... Kend-all had said she was always here by eleven-thirty. She had to be to do the things she had to do. And she'd have to race to do it. She'd have to take all the shortcuts.

I jerked the alley gate open, and looked up the line of high board fence. I looked just as she turned into the alley, pulling herself along on the fence, using the crutch as a cane.

For a moment I was sicker than I'd been when I first got up. Then, the sickness went away, gave way to anger. I ran to meet her, cursing the whole world and everybody in it.

"For Christ's sake, honey!" I took the crutch out of her hand, and drew her arm around my shoulder. "Are you hurt? Stop a minute and get your br—"

"N-no!" she panted. "J-just let me l-lean on you s-so—"

Her face was smudged, and the left side of her coat was all dusty and dirty. Apparently the end piece of the crutch had worked loose, and she'd taken a hell of a fall.

"Where did it happen?" I said. "Why didn't you ask someone for help? My God, baby, you shouldn't—"

"H-hurry," she gasped. "Please, C-carl."

I hurried, letting her use me as a crutch. And I didn't ask any more foolish questions. What difference did it make where the accident had happened, whether she'd been struggling for two blocks or six—two thousand miles or six thousand?

I got her across the back yard and up the steps. Hurrying, hurrying, the two of us one person. And her pounding heart, pounding so hard that it seemed to come right out through the skin, was my pounding heart.

I helped her into the kitchen and pushed her into a chair. She struggled to get up, and I pushed her down into it hard.

"Stay there!" I said. "Goddammit, stay there! If you don't sit still, by God I'll slough you!"

"I c-can't! Mrs. W-winroy—"

"Listen to me!" I said. "Will you listen, Ruth? Everything's going to be all right."

"It w-won't!" She was rocking in the chair, weeping help-lessly. "Y-you don't understand. Y-you don't know how it is. She'll f-fire me, and I j-just can't—I've g-got t-to—"

I slapped her across the face, two quick hard slaps with the palm of my hand and the back of it.

"Want to listen?" I drew my hand back, ready to swing at her again. "Just tell me what you want to do. You want to listen or do I knock your head right off of your shoulders?"

"I—I'm"—she shuddered and gulped down a sob—"I'm l-listening, Carl."

I found the whiskey bottle in the cupboard and poured out a

stiff shot. I stood over her, watching her to see that she drank every last drop.

"Better, huh?" I grinned. "Now you're going to eat something, and then you're going to lie down."

"No! I—"

"You have to be at school this afternoon? Have to? Sure, you don't, and you're not going to. Everything's jake here. No one showed for lunch but Kendall and he won't say anything. I'll talk to him and see that he doesn't."

"Y-you don't know! Mrs. Winroy—"

"She went downtown to get some money. She'll get it if she has to take it out of Winroy's hide, and after she gets it she'll have to spend it. She won't be home for a long time. I know, get me? I know exactly what she'll do."

"B-but"—she looked at me, curiously, a faint frown on her face—"I h-have to make—"

"Make the beds. What else?"

"Well. P-pick up the rooms a little."

"What time do you usually get out of school?"

"Four."

"Well, today maybe you cut a class. See what I mean? If she gets home before I think she will. You're home early, and you're hard at it when she gets here. Okay?"

"But I have to—"

"I'll do it," I said. "And don't tell me I can't. I'm a whiz at making beds and picking up. Now, I'll fix you a little lunch and help you upstairs, and—"

"No, Carl! Just—just do the other. I'll fix my own lunch. Honest, I will. I'll do anything you say, but p-please—"

"How are you going to do it? What about your crutch?"

"I'll fix it! I've done it before. I can tighten the screws with a case knife, and there's some tape here and—Please, Carl!"

I didn't argue with her. It was better to let her do a little something than to have her go hysterical again.

I gave her the crutch and a knife and the roll of tape.

There were two bedrooms downstairs, Ruth's and an unoccupied one—I didn't have to bother with them, of course. Upstairs there were four bedrooms, or, I should say, four rooms with beds in them. Because you couldn't call the place Jake slept a real bedroom. It was more like a long, narrow closet, barely big enough for a bed and a chair and a lopsided chest of drawers. I guessed it had been a closet before Fay Winroy had stopped sleeping with him.

Since he hadn't slept there the night before, there wasn't much of anything to do to it. Nothing at all, in fact. But I went in and looked around—after I'd put my gloves on.

There was a half-empty fifth of port on the chest of drawers. Six-bits a bottle stuff. In the top drawer of the chest was a small white prescription box. I rocked it a little with the tip of one finger. I studied the label. *Amyt. 5 gr. NO MORE THAN ONE IN ANY SIX HOUR PERIOD.*

Five-grain amytal. Goofballs. Tricky stuff. You take one, and you forget that you've done it. So you take more...A few of those in that rotgut wine, and—?

Nothing. Not good enough. He might drink too little, and

you'd only tip your hand. He might toss down too much, and throw it up.

No, it wasn't good enough, but the basic idea was sound. It would have to be something like that, something that could logically happen to him because of what he was.

In the bottom drawer, there was a forty-five with a sawed-off barrel.

I looked it over, moving it with my finger tips, and saw that it was cleaned and loaded. I closed the drawer and left the room.

You didn't really have to aim that gun for close-range shooting. All you had to do was pull the trigger and let it spray. And if you happen to be cleaning it when...

Huh-uh. It was too obvious. Whenever a man's killed with something that's made for killing—well, you see what I mean. People get ideas even where there's nothing to get ideas about.

Mrs. Winroy's room looked like a cyclone had struck it; it looked like she might have tried to see how big a mess she could make. I did a particularly good job on it, and went on to Mr. Kendall's room.

Everything there was about as you'd expect it to be. Clothes all hung up. Bookcases stretching along one side of the room and halfway down another. About the only thing out of place was a book lying across the arm of an easy chair.

I picked it up after I'd finished doing the little work that had to be done, and saw that it was something called *Mr. Blettsworthy on Rampole Island* by H.G. Wells. I read a few paragraphs at the place where it had been left open. It was about a guy who'd been picked up by a bunch of savages, and they were holding him prisoner down in a kind of canyon. And he was pretty worried about getting to be as crummy as they were, but he was more worried about something else. Just staying alive. I only ready those few paragraphs, like I've said, but I could see how it was going to turn out. When it came to a choice of being nice and dead or crummy and alive, the guy would work overtime at being a heel.

I crossed the hall to my own room. I was just finishing it up when I heard Ruth coming up the stairs.

She looked in all the other rooms first, making sure, I guess, that I'd done them up right.

I asked her how she was feeling. She said, "J-just fine," and, "C-carl, I can't tell you how much I—"

"What's the use trying, then?" I grinned. "Come on, now, and I'll help you downstairs. I want you to get some rest before Mrs. Winroy shows up."

"But I'm all—I don't need any—"

"I think you do," I said. "You still look a little shaky to me."

I took her back downstairs, making her put most of her weight on me. I made her lie down on her bed, and I sat down on the edge of it. And there wasn't anything more I could do for her, and I couldn't think of anything to say. But she lay there, looking at me as though she expected something more; and when I started to get up she put her hand over mine.

6

I think I'd better shove off," I said. "I want to tell Mr. Kendall not to say anything about missing his lunch."

"C-arl. Do you —?"

"What about him, anyway?" I said. "How long has he been boarding here?"

"Well" — she hesitated — "not very long. They didn't start keeping boarders until this last fall."

"And he moved in right away?"

"Well — yes. I mean, I think he was the one who gave them the idea of running a boarding house. You see, the way it is here, in a college town, you can't have both girls and boys — men — living in the same place. So the place where he was living, all the boarders were boys and they were awfully noisy, I guess, and —"

"I see. The Winroys had plenty of room, so he asked them to take him in. And as long as they had the one boarder, they decided to go after some others."

"Uh-huh. Only no one else would stay with them. I guess Mr. Kendall knew it would never be crowded here."

"Yeah," I said. "I imagine he did. Well, I think I'll go and see him, and—"

"Carl." Her hand tightened on mine. "About last...I'm not sorry, Carl."

"All right," I said, trying to be firm and gentle at the same time. "I'm glad you're not sorry, Ruthie, and there's nothing for you to worry about. Now let's just leave it at that, huh? Let's make like it never happened."

"B-but I—I thought—"

"It's better that way, Ruthie. Mrs. Winroy might catch on. I've got an idea she wouldn't like it."

"B-but she didn't last night. If w-we were careful and—"

She was blushing; she couldn't look at me straight.

"Look," I said, "that stuff won't get you anything, kid. Nothing but trouble. You were doing all right before, weren't you? Well, then—"

"Tell me something, Carl. Is it because of my—because I'm like I am?"

"I've told you why," I said. "It's just damned bad business. I haven't got anything. I don't know how long I'm going to be here. You can't win, know what I mean? You ought to be doing your stepping out with one of the local boys—some nice steady guy you can marry some day and give you the kind of life you ought to have."

She bit her lip, turning her head on the pillows until she was staring at the wall.

"Yes," she said, slowly. "I suppose that's what I'd better do. Start stepping out. Get married. Thank you."

"Look," I said. "All I'm trying to do is—"

"It's my fault, Carl. I felt different around you. You seemed to like me, and you didn't seem to notice how—notice anything. And I guess I thought it was because you—I don't mean there's anything wrong with you—but—"

"I know," I said. "I felt the same way."

"And"—she didn't seem to have heard me—"you were just trying to be nice, weren't you?"

"Ruth," I said.

"It's all right, Carl. Thanks for everything. You'd better go, now."

I didn't go, of course. I couldn't after that. I lay down at her side, pulling her around facing me, holding her when she tried to pull away. And after a moment, she stopped trying; she was holding me twice as hard.

"Don't go away, Carl! Promise you won't go away! I've n-never had anyone, and if you went away I—"

"I won't," I said. "Not for a long time, anyway. I'm going to stay right here, Ruthie."

"Was it g-g—" She was whispering, whispering and shivering, her face pressed close to mine. "Did you l-like—me?"

"I—Look," I said. "I just don't think—"

"Please, Carl. P-please!" she said, and slowly she turned her body under mine. And there was just one way of telling her that it was all right.

It was all right. It was better than all right. I didn't look down at that little baby foot, and nothing could have been any better.

We went up to the bathroom together. Then I left the house and headed for the bakery.

It was a long one-story, buff brick building, about a block and a half up the street toward the business section. I passed up the offices, and went around to the side where a couple of guys were loading bread into trucks.

"Mr. Kendall?" One of them jerked his head at the side door. "He's probably in on the floor. Just keep going until you spot him."

I went in. I went down a long corridor, crowded with wire racks of bread, and came out into a big room where about fifty guys were working. Some of them where throwing long ropes of dough over hooks in the wall, throwing it and pulling it back and throwing it again. And others were carrying the dough away from the hooks and laying it out on long wooden tables.

One side of the room was made up of a row of brick ovens, and the guys working in front of them were stripped to the waist. They'd flick the door of the oven open, and reach inside with a kind of flat-bladed shovel; they'd reach about sixty times to the second, it looked like. I was watching them, thinking that that kind of work I could do without, when Mr. Kendall came up behind me.

"Well," he said, touching me on the arm. "What do you think of us, Mr. Bigelow?"

"It's quite a place," I said.

"Not completely modern," he said. "I mean, it's not mechanized to the extent that big-city bakeries are. But with help so cheap there's no reason why it should be."

I nodded. "I came over to explain about Ruth, Mr. Kendall. She had an accident on the way home at noon, and—"

"An accident! Was she badly hurt?"

"Just shaken up. Her crutch gave way under her, and she took a spill."

"The poor child! You're not in any hurry? Well, let's get out of this noise for a moment."

I followed him across the room, a fussy polite little guy in white overalls and a white sailor cap.

We entered another room, about a third of the size of the first one, and he pushed the connecting door shut. He boosted himself up on a table and gestured for me to sit beside him.

"It's clean, Mr. Bigelow. We don't keep flour in here, just the more or less precious commodities. Looks a little like a grocery store, doesn't it, with all these shelves?"

"Yeah," I said. "Now, about Ruth. I wanted to ask you—"

"You don't need to, Mr. Bigelow." He took out his pipe and began filling it. "Naturally, I won't say anything to Mrs. Winroy. But thank you for letting me know what the situation was."

"That's all right," I said. "I helped her set the rooms straight. I mean—"

I let my voice trail away, cursing myself. I didn't want anyone to know that I'd been through the rooms.

"Mmm," he nodded absent-mindedly. "I'm very glad you came over, Mr. Bigelow. As I said at noon. I don't want to appear presumptuous, but I've been thinking—uh—don't you believe that, instead of merely waiting around until you hear from the sheriff, it might be well for you to start putting roots down? In a word, don't you feel it would be sound psychology to demonstrate that there is not the slightest doubt in your own mind of the outcome of last night's unfortunate business?"

"Yeah?" I said. "I don't get you."

"I was referring to—" He paused. "Now that—your response just now—brings up something else I wanted to speak to you about. If, that is, you won't think I'm—uh—being—"

"Let's say, I won't," I said. "You're not being presumptuous. You just feel a friendly interest in me, and you want to give me a little fatherly advice."

I'd said it the right way, and there wasn't anything in my face to show that I didn't mean it.

"I'm glad you understand, Mr. Bigelow. To take the second matter first, I was going to suggest that you be a little more careful about the language you use. I know most young men talk rather slangily and—uh—tough these days, and no one thinks anything of it. But in your case, well, don't you see?"

"I understand. And I appreciate the advice," I said. "After all, regardless of what's happened, it won't hurt me to talk a little better brand of English."

"I'm afraid I put things rather badly," he said. "Badly or baldly, if there's any difference, I suppose I'm so used to ordering these student workers around that—"

"Sure—surely," I said. "Don't apologize, Mr. Kendall. Like I say, I appreciate your interest."

"It's a very warm interest, Mr. Bigelow." He bobbed his head seriously. "All my life, I've had someone to look after, and now with my parents dead—God rest them—and nothing to occupy me but my job and my books, I—I—"

"Sure. Surely," I repeated.

He laughed, a shamed sad little laugh. "I tried to take a vacation last year. I own a little lakeside cabin up in Canada—nothing pretentious, you understand; the site is too isolated to have any value, and we, my father and I, built the cabin ourselves—so I bought a car and started to drive up there. Two days after I left town, I was back here again. Back here working. And I've hardly had my car out of the garage since."

I nodded, waiting. He chuckled halfheartedly. "That's an explanation and an apology, if you can unravel it. Incidentally, if you'd like to use the car some time, you'll be entirely welcome."

"Thanks," I said. "I'd be glad to pay you for it."

"You'd only complicate my life further for me." He laughed again. "I could only add it to my savings, and since they, obviously, can do me not the slightest good—I couldn't appreciate the pleasures they might buy, and the pension which will soon be due me is more than enough to provide for my wants—so—"

I said, "I understand," or something equally brilliant.

"I imagine I'm too old to acquire the habit of spending," he went on. "Thrift like work has become a vice with me. I'm not comfortable with them, but I'd be less content without them. Does that sound pretty stupid to you?"

"I wouldn't put it that way," I said. "I'd say, though, that if you had *enough* money—you know twenty or thirty thousand dollars—you might get quite a bit of fun out of it."

"Mmm. You feel the case is similar to that of having a little knowledge, eh? Perhaps you're right. But since the relative little is what I do have and I see no way of substantially increasing it—" He ended the sentence with a shrug. "Now to get back to you, Mr. Bigelow, if I may—if you won't feel that I'm trying to order your life for you—"

"Not at all," I said.

"I've felt for a long time that there should be a storeroom man in here. Someone to check these supplies out instead of merely letting the different departments help themselves. I mentioned the fact to the owner today and he gave his approval, so if you'd like to have the job you can start in immediately."

"And you think I should?" I said. "Start in immediately, I mean."

"Well"—he hesitated; then he nodded firmly—"I certainly don't see that you could lose anything by it."

I lighted a cigarette, stalling for a minute's time. I thought it over fast, and I decided that whatever he was or wasn't, I was on my own. This was my job, my game, and I knew how to play it. And if anyone was going to tell me what to do, it would have to be The Man.

"I'll tell you what, Mr. Kendall," I said. "I've had a long trip, and I'm pretty tired and—"

"The job won't be at all arduous. You can set your own hours, practically, and much of the time there's nothing at all to—"

"I think I'd rather wait," I said. "I plan on running into New York tomorrow night, or Saturday at the latest. Today would probably be the only day I could get in before Sunday."

"Oh," he said. "Well, of course, in that case—"

70

"I would like to have the job, though," I said. "That is, if you can hold it for me."

He said that he could, rather reluctantly, apparently not too pleased at failing to get his own way. Then his face cleared suddenly, and he slid down off the table.

"I can give it to you, now," he said. "We'll say that you're just laying off for a couple of days."

"Fine," I said.

"I know I'm overcautious and apprehensive. But I always feel that if there's any small barrier we can erect against potential difficulties we should take advantage of it."

"Perhaps you're right," I said.

We walked along the rows of shelves, with him pointing out the different cans and packages of baking ingredients and giving me a running commentary on how they were used.

"I'm having some batch cards designed — that is, requisitions for ingredients which the various departments will submit to you. All you'll have to do is fill them. Now, over here is our cold-storage room where we keep perishables —"

He levered the door on a big walk-in refrigerator, the kind you see in meat markets, and we went inside. "Egg whites," he said, tapping a fifteen-gallon can with the toe of his shoe. "And these are egg yolks, and here are whole eggs," tapping two more cans. "Bakeries buy these things this way for two reasons: they're considerably cheaper, of course, and they can be measured much more easily."

"I see," I said, trying to keep from shivering. I'd only been in the place for a minute, but the cold was cutting me to the bone.

"Now, this door," he said, pushing it open again. "You'll notice that I left it well off the latch. I'd suggest that you do the same if you don't want to risk freezing to death. As"—he smiled pleasantly—"I'm sure you don't."

"You can sing two choruses of that," I said, following him out of the refrigerator. "I mean—"

He laughed and gave me a dignified clap on the back. "Quite all right, Mr. Bigelow. As I said a moment ago, I'm inclined to be overcautious...Well, I think that will be enough for today. Uh—I know it isn't much, but in view of the job's other advantages—uh—will twelve dollars a week be all right?"

"That will be fine," I said.

"You can set your own hours—within reason. The ingredients for the various dough batches can be checked out before they're ready for use, and then you'll be free to study or do—uh—anything else you like."

We left the main storage room and entered a smaller one, an anteroom, stacked high with sacks of salt, sugar and flour. At the end of a narrow corridor between the sacks, there was a door opening onto the street. Kendall unlocked it, winking at me.

"You see, Mr. Bigelow? Your own private entrance and exit. No one is supposed to have a key to this but me, but if you should be caught up on your work and feel the need for a breath of air, I see no reason why—uh—"

He gave me one of his prim, dignified smiles, and let me out the door. I paused outside and lighted another cigarette, glancing casually up and down the street. The door—the one I'd just come out of—was well to the right of the entrance to the office.

Even if there was someone in there working late, as I would be on an after-school job, I could go in and out without being seen. And straight down the street, a matter of a hundred and fifty yards or so, was the house.

With Fay Winroy to set him up for a certain time—a good dark night—it would be a cinch. I could stand there at the door and watch until he went by, and then...

It was too much pie. It was so good that I couldn't make up my mind whether I liked it.

I sauntered on down the street, turning in at the bar across from the house. I ordered an ale, and sat down.

Kendall. Was he just a nice old busybody, a man who'd taken a fancy to me like a lot of elderly people had, or had The Man got to him? I couldn't make up my mind about him. Twice now, well, three times, I'd thought I'd had him figured. And each time, even now, right after he'd practically told me where he stood and handed me the deal on a platter, I began to doubt my figuring. I still wasn't sure.

He just didn't fit the part. No matter what he said or did, I just couldn't hold a picture of him as a guy who'd get mixed up in a gang murder. And yet... well, you see? That was what made him an almost sure-fire bet. If— *if* The Man was a little leery of me, *if* he did have an ace in the hole—little old man Kendall would be his boy. It would have to be him or someone like him.

I kicked it around in my mind, pulling myself first one way then the other...Whatever he was, Kendall was a long way from being stupid. He wouldn't do the job himself, assuming that it was something that an amateur could handle. He wouldn't work with me as an accomplice. He'd handle his end without doing a thing that could be pinned on him. And if I didn't handle mine, if I fell down on the job or screwed it up...

I didn't like to think about it. Because if I fell down or screwed it up, I'd never live to fumble another one. Maybe I wouldn't, anyway, but I'd have a chance. I'd done the vanishing act before, and I'd stayed hidden for more than six years. But with Kendall keeping tabs on me—if he *was*—with him tipping off The Man the moment I went sour on the deal or it went sour on me...

Huh-uh. The Man didn't take excuses. He didn't let you quit. I wouldn't run far enough to work up a sweat.

I bought another ale. So what if it was that way? I'd agreed to do the job, and as long as I did it I'd be all right. Since that was the way things stood, what difference did it make about Kendall?

It made plenty. It showed that The Man didn't trust me—and it wasn't good when The Man didn't trust you. It was either that or he was leery of the job—and that wasn't good either. The Man didn't operate on hunches. If he was leery, he had good reason to be.

I wondered what he'd say if I asked him point-blank about Kendall. And I didn't need to wonder long about it; I was through wondering almost before I began.

He'd laugh it off. He'd put his arm around my shoulder and tell me how much he liked me...and that would be the beginning of a damned fast end. He'd have to get rid of me. He'd be afraid not to. Afraid I might be getting panicky or worrying about a double-cross.

I finished my ale, and started out of the bar. Just as I reached the door, Fay Winroy came in.

"Oh, there you are, hon—" she caught herself. "I thought you might be over here. The sher—there's someone at the house to see you."

She drew me outside, lowering her voice. "It's the sheriff, honey. Maybe you'd better go on over by yourself, and I'll stay here for a drink."

"All right," I said. "Thanks for hunting me up."

"Carl"—she looked at me anxiously—"are you sure that everything's all right? Is there anything that—?"

"Not a thing," I said. "Why?"

"Nothing. No reason. He said it was all right, but—"

"Yeah?" I said.

"He acts so funny about it, Carl. So...so awfully funny—"

7

He was waiting for me in the living room. When I came in, he eased himself up out of his chair a few inches, as though he was planning on shaking hands. Then, he let himself down again, and I sat down across from him.

"I'm sorry I kept you waiting," I said. "I've been down at the bakery lining up a part-time job."

"Uh-hah," he nodded. "Miss Ruth told me she thought you might be there, but you was already gone when I stopped by. Got you a job, eh?"

"Yes, sir," I said. "I haven't started to work yet, but—"

"Uh-hah. You're plannin' on staying here, then? Going to school and all."

"Why, yes," I said. "That's why I came here."

"Uh-hah, sure," he drawled again. "Well, I hope it works out all right. We got a nice little town here. Nice little college. We'd like to keep it that way."

I frowned at him, looking him straight in the eye. "I don't particularly like it here, sheriff," I said. "In fact, I wish I'd never seen your town or your college. But now that I'm here I plan on staying. And if you can think of any reason why I shouldn't, perhaps you'd better tell me."

He swallowed heavily. He wasn't used to being talked to that way. "Didn't say there was any reason, did I? Maybe you better tell me if you can think of any."

I didn't even bother to answer him.

He cleared his throat, uncomfortably. After a moment, his glance wavered and he gave me a sheepish grin. "Pshaw," he mumbled. "Now how the heck did I ever get started talkin' to you that-a-way? Must be I had to hold in the good news I had for you so long it kinda clabbered on me. Ever have that happen to you? You got somethin' nice to pass on to a fella, and when you can't find him—"

"Good news?" I said. "What good news?"

"The answers to them wires I sent to Arizona. Don't know when I've seen so many good things said about a man. Looked like the judge an' the chief o' police was trying to outdo each other."

"They're very fine gentlemen," I said.

"Must be. Don't see how they could be anything else," he nodded firmly. "And with two high-placed people like that speakin' up for you, I don't see—"

"Yes?" I said.

"Nothin'. Just sort of talkin' to myself, more or less. Kind of a bad habit of mine." He stood up, slapping his hat against the side of his pants. "Let's see, now. You was saying you planned on running into the city this weekend?"

"Tomorrow or Saturday," I said. "If it's all right."

"Sure, sure it's all right. You just go right ahead."

He put out his hand, and gave mine a firm hard grip.

I went upstairs and my head had hardly touched the pillows before Fay Winroy slipped into the room.

"Carl. Was it—what did he want?"

"Nothing much." I moved over on the bed to let her sit down. "Just came to tell me that I'd gotten a clean bill from Arizona."

"Oh? But he acted so strange, Carl. I thought—"

"How about it?" I said. "You didn't give him a bad time when he came here looking for me."

"N-no." She hesitated. "I mean, naturally I don't like cops hanging around with their cars parked in front of the house, but—well, I'm sure I didn't say anything out of the way."

I wouldn't have bet money on it. "I don't imagine Kendall liked having him come to the bakery, either," I said. "That must have been the trouble. The guy had his feelings hurt."

"You can't think of anything else?"

I shrugged. "I don't know what it would be. How did you make out with Jake?"

Her eyes flashed. "I don't want to talk about him."

"Neither do I," I yawned. "In fact, I'd just as soon not talk at all. I think I'll take a nap."

"Well," she laughed, getting up. "Here's my hat, what's my hurry, huh? But it's almost dinnertime, honey."

"I'm not hungry," I said.

"You could have something up here. Would you like to have me bring you up a tray in about an hour?"

"Well—" I frowned.

"It'll be all right. Kendall will be gone back to the bakery — you'd think the guy would move his bed over there — and Ruth will have plenty to keep her busy in the kitchen. I'll see that she does."

I nodded. "In about an hour, then."

She left. I closed my eyes and tried to forget about Kendall, and the sheriff, and The Man and Fruit Jar and . . .

I was still trying an hour later when she pushed the door open and came in with the tray.

She had a glass half full of whiskey on it, covered up with a napkin. I drank it down, and began to feel hungry.

It was a good dinner — a beef stew with vegetables, and apple pie for dessert. Fay lay back on the bed while I ate, her hands clasped under the back of her head.

I drank the last of my coffee. I lay down crosswise on the bed with her, pulling her around in my arms.

"Carl —"

"That's me," I said.

"Did you really mean what you said this morning? About us — me — going into New York?"

I reached the wallet out of my pocket, and took out two twenties. I tucked them into the front of her brassiere.

"Oh, Carl, honey," she sighed. "I can hardly wait."

I told her where to meet me, a hotel on West Forty-seventh where the fix was in strong.

"I'll go in tomorrow afternoon," I said, "and come back late Saturday night. You come in Saturday morning, and come back here Sunday night. And don't forget to fix things up with your sister."

79

"I won't, honey!" She sat up eagerly. "I'll be very careful about everything. I'll tell Jake that sis sent me the money to come on, and—"

"All right," I said. "Just be careful, and let it go at that."

She took the bills out of her brassiere, and smoothed them over her knee. Then, she folded them neatly and tucked them back between her breasts.

"Sweet," she said, huskily, laying her head against my shoulder. "You don't mind waiting, do you, honey?"

I didn't mind. I wanted it—who the hell wouldn't have—but I wasn't in any hurry. It was something that had to be done, the clincher to the bargain.

"It would do me good to mind?" I said.

"Yes," she nodded. "I'm not—well, I know I'm a long way from being what I should be—but here, well, to do it—to start off here in Jake's house...If you say so, I will but—"

"That's okay," I said.

"You're not sore, Carl? You know what I'm trying to say?"

"I think I do," I said, "and it's all right. But I can't say how long it will stay that way if you don't beat it out of here."

She looked at me teasingly, her head cocked a little to one side.

"Suppose I change my mind," she said. "Suppose I wake up in the night, and—"

I made a grab for her. She leaped back, laughing, and ran to the door. She pursed her lips; then she whispered, "Good night, honey," and slipped out of the room.

...I slept pretty good that night. Nothing out of the way

happened the next morning. I got up around nine, after Kendall and Ruth had left, and fixed my own breakfast. I lingered over it, thinking Fay might join me, but she didn't. So I cleaned up the dishes, left for the railroad station.

The Long Island was outdoing itself that day. It was only an hour late getting into New York. I picked up the suit I'd bought and checked in at the hotel. At six o'clock I called The Man from a booth telephone. Then I strolled down to the Automat near Forty-second and Broadway and waited.

Fruit Jar drove up in front of the place at seven o'clock. I got into the Cadillac, and we headed for The Man's house.

8

You've heard of The Man. Everyone has. There's hardly a month passes that the papers don't have a story about him or you don't see his picture. One month he's up before some government investigating committee. The next he's attending a big political dinner — laughing and talking to some of the very same people who were putting him through the wringer the month before.

The Man is a big importer. He controls shipping companies, and distilleries, race tracks and jobbing houses, wire services and loan companies.

He's one of the biggest open-shop employers in the country, but it's not because he's opposed to unions. He's a charter member of two old-line craft unions, and he's supported their organizational drives, and he's got letters from some of the top labor-skates thanking him for his "earnest endeavors in behalf of the American workingman."

The Man controls race tracks — but he supports anti-racetrack legislation. He can prove that he's supported it, and you can't prove that he controls the tracks. He controls distilleries — but can you prove it?—and he supports temperance movements. He controls loan companies—controls the men who control them—and he backs anti-loan-shark laws.

The Man donated heavily to the defense of the Scottsboro boys. The Man went bail for bigwigs in the Klan.

No one has ever pinned anything on him.

He's too big, too powerful, too covered-up. You try to pin something on him, and you lose it along the way.

The Man lived in a big stone and brick house out in Forest Hills. He wasn't married, of course—although I don't know why I say of course—and the only servant around was the square-faced Japanese houseboy who let us in.

The boy took us into the library-drawing room where The Man was waiting. And The Man still stood beaming at me, shaking my hand and asking me about my trip East and saying how delighted he was to meet me.

"I'm so sorry I didn't get to talk to you before you went down to Peardale," he said, in his soft pleasant voice. "Not, I'm sure, that you need my advice."

"I thought I'd better not lose any more time," I said. "The school term has already started."

"Of course. Naturally." He finally let go of my hand and waved me to a chair. "You're here, now, and that's the important thing."

He sat down, smiling, and nodded to Fruit Jar. "Perfect, wouldn't you say so, Murph? We couldn't have found a better man for the job than Little Bigger. Didn't I tell you he'd be worth any trouble we went to in locating him?"

Fruit Jar grunted.

"Would you mind telling me how you did it?" I said. "How you found me?"

"Not at all. But I didn't suppose it would be anything that would mystify you."

"Well, it doesn't exactly," I said. "I mean, I think I have it figured out. I was red hot here in the East, and I'd had a little lung trouble—"

"And your teeth and eyes were very bad."

"You figured I'd just about have to go West. I'd have to take some kind of unskilled outdoors job. I'd get my teeth and my eyes taken care of—not in the place I was living but some place nearby—and I'd be damned careful to build up a good reputation. And—and—"

"About all, isn't it?" He chuckled, beaming at me. "The teeth and the contact lenses, of course, were decisive."

"But the police knew as much about me as you did. Even more, maybe. If you could find me, why couldn't they?"

"Ah, the police," he said. "Poor fellows. So many distractions and diversions and restrictions. So many things to do and so little to do it with."

"There's the reward money. It totaled around forty-seven thousand dollars the last I heard."

"But, my dear Charlie! We can't expend public funds on the off-chance that the police may collect rewards. Of course if they wished to carry on their search on their own time and at their own expense—"

"Yeah," I said, "but—"

"Some ambitious private investigator? No, Charlie. I can understand the slight trepidation which you may feel, but it is absolutely groundless. What would it profit anyone—some reward-hungry or public-spirited citizen—if he did find you? He would have to prove your identity, would he not? And who would believe that you, this soft-spoken slip of a youth, was a murderer? You've never been arrested, never mugged or fingerprinted."

I nodded. He spread his hands, smiling.

"You see, Charlie? I didn't need to prove who you were. With me it was merely necessary to know. I could then place my proposition before you and ask for your co-operation—I dislike the word demand don't you?—and you were kind enough to give it. The police, the courts"—he shrugged wryly—"Paah!"

"I'd like to get just one more thing straight," I said. "I wanted this job, but I don't want any others. I don't want to pick up again where I left off the last time."

"Naturally, you don't. What...Murph, didn't you tell him?"

"Not more than a dozen times," said Fruit Jar.

The Man gave him a long, slow look. He turned back to me. "You have my word on it, Charlie. It wouldn't be practical to use you again, even if I wanted to."

"Fine," I said, "that's all I wanted to know."

"I'm delighted to reassure you. Now, to get down to the business at hand—"

I gave him a report on how things stacked up in Peardale—about my run-in with Jake and lining up a job at the bakery and how I'd made out with the sheriff. He seemed pleased. He kept nodding and smiling, and saying "Excellent" and "Splendid" and so on.

Then he asked me one question, and for a moment I was kind of stunned. I felt my face turning red.

"Well?" He asked it again. "You said the sheriff got his report on you yesterday afternoon. Did Jake stay at the house last night?"

"I"—I swallowed—"I don't believe he did."

"You don't *believe* he did? Don't you know?"

I should have known, of course. It was the one thing I should have known. I was pretty sure that he hadn't stayed at the house but I'd been worn out and I'd got to grab-assing around with Fay Winroy and...

"That's rather important," The Man said. And waited. "If he wasn't there last night, how can you be sure that he plans on staying there at all?"

"Well," I said, "I—I don't think—"

"You can say that again!" Fruit Jar snickered. "Boy, oh, boy!" That snapped me out of it.

"Look," I said. "Look, sir. I talked to the sheriff yesterday for the second time in two days. I spent more than an hour with this man Kendall. He doesn't know anything but he's a pretty sharp old bird—"

"Kendall? Oh, yes, the baker. I see no cause to worry about him."

"I'm not worried about him or the sheriff either. But with Jake feeling the way he does, I don't have to move very far out of line to be in trouble. I can't show any interest in him. I can't do anything that might be interpreted as showing interest in him. I deliberately went to bed early last night, and I stayed there until late this morning. I—"

"Yes, yes," The Man interrupted impatiently. "I commend you for your discretion. But there should have been some way to—"

"He'll stay at the house," I said. "Mrs. Winroy will see that he does."

"Oh?"

"Yes."

He shook his head, leaning forward in his chair. "Not just yes, Charlie. Are you telling me that after only forty-eight hours, you've made a proposition to Mrs. Winroy?"

"I've been leading up to one, and she'll grab it. She hates Jake's guts. She'll jump at the chance to get rid of him and make herself a stake at the same time."

"I'm relieved that you think so. Personally, I believe I'd have taken a little more time in arriving at such a decision."

"I couldn't take any more time. She was opening up to me before I'd talked to her five minutes. If I hadn't played up to her right at the start, I might not have got another chance."

"So? And you felt you had to have her assistance?"

"I think it will come in pretty handy, yes. She can still make Jake jump through hoops. She knows her way around. She could get tough if she thought she was losing her meal ticket with nothing to take the place of it."

"Well," The Man sighed. "I can only hope your appraisal is correct. I believe she's a former actress, isn't she?"

"A singer."

"Singer, actress. The two arts overlap."

"I've got her taped," I said. "I've only known her a couple of days, but I've known women like her all my life."

"Mmm. May I assume that there's a connection between her and your arrival in town a day early?"

"She's meeting me here tomorrow. She's supposed to be visiting her sister, but—"

"I understand. Well, I'm rather sorry you didn't consult me, but inasmuch as you didn't—"

"I thought that was why you wanted me," I said. "Because I'd know what to do without being told."

"Oh, I did, Charlie. I do." He smiled quickly. "I don't at all doubt your ability and judgment. It's just that your procedure seemed rather daring—unorthodox—for such an extremely important matter."

"It seems that way here. Other things may seem that way to you. Here. What I have to go on is how things seem to me there. It's the only way I can work. If I had to ask you every time I wanted to make a move—well, I just couldn't do it. I—I'm not telling you where to get off, but—"

"Of course not," he nodded warmly. "After all, we're all intent on the same goal. We're all friends. We all have a great deal to gain...or lose. You understand that part don't you, Charlie? Murph made it clear to you?"

"He did, but he didn't need to."

"Good. Now, about the time. You'll naturally be governed to an extent by the local factors, but the optimum date would be about a week before the trial. That will allow you to become firmly integrated into the life of the town, to allay the suspicion which always attaches to a stranger. Also, by disposing of Jake at the approximate time of the trial, the newspapers will have less to feed upon; there will only be one story instead of two."

"I'll try to handle it that way," I said.

"Fine. Splendid. Now...Oh, yes"—his smile faded—"one more thing. Murph tells me that you pulled a knife on him. Actually stabbed him in the back of the neck."

"He shouldn't have been there in Peardale. You know he shouldn't, sir."

"Perhaps not. But that doesn't excuse your actions. I don't like that at all, Charlie." He shook his head sternly.

I looked down at the floor and kept my mouth shut.

"Would you mind waiting out in the reception room, Murph? I have quite a few things to say to Charlie."

"I don't mind," said Fruit Jar. "Take your time." And he sauntered out of the room, grinning.

The Man chuckled softly, and I looked up. He was holding out the knife to me.

"Could you use it again, Charlie?"

I stared at him—pretty blankly, I guess. He put the knife in my hand and closed my fingers around it.

"You killed his brother," he said. "Did you know that?"

"Christ no!" So that was it! "When—what—?"

"I don't know the details. It was in Detroit, 1942, I believe."

Detroit, 1942. I tried to place him, and of course I couldn't. The name wouldn't have meant anything. And there'd been four—no, five in Detroit.

"I was disturbed by the way he felt toward you. I made a few inquiries... It won't do, Charlie. He's stupid and vengeful. He could blow things higher than a kite."

"Yeah," I said, "but... tonight?"

"Tonight. You haven't been here, Charlie. He was here to see me about a financial matter. I walked out to the car with him when he left. I saw him stop down there on the highway and pick up a hitchhiker. In fact, Toko and I both saw him."

He chuckled again.

"You understand my position, Charlie? I depended on Murph, and he failed me. How long would I last if I tolerated failure in the people I depend upon? I simply can't do it, Charlie, regardless of the person or cost. The whole system is based on swift punishment and prompt reward."

"I understand," I said.

"In that case—" He stood up. "How about another drink before you leave?"

"I guess not," I said. "I mean, no, thanks, sir."

He walked out to the car with Fruit Jar and me, walked between us with an arm around each of our shoulders. He shook hands with both of us, and stood at the side of the car talking a moment.

"A beautiful evening," he said, breathing in deep. "Smell that air, Charlie? I'll bet Arizona doesn't have anything finer than that."

"No, sir," I said.

"I know. There's no place like Arizona, is there? Well—" He gave Fruit Jar a playful punch on the arm. "Why don't I see more of you these days, hey? Not for business. Just a little quiet get-together?"

"Well, say" — Fruit Jar began to puff up — "just say the word, and —"

"We'll make it Sunday... No, no I'll come to see you." He stepped back from the car beaming. "Sunday afternoon, say. I'll look forward to it —"

Fruit Jar drove away, so swelled up that he could hardly sit behind the wheel. And I wanted to burst out laughing. Or crying. Because he was a no-good son-of-a-bitch, but I felt sorry for him.

"I guess you got told off," he said, flicking a glance at me. "You're lucky he didn't do nothin' but eat you out."

"He told me off," I said. "I'm lucky."

"You think me'n him ain't like that? You think he didn't mean that about coming to see me?"

I shook my head. The Man would see him all right. He'd have a quiet get-together with him Sunday afternoon.

They'd have Fruit Jar embalmed by that time.

9

The trouble with killing is that it's so easy. You get to where you almost do it without thinking. You do it instead of thinking.

...I told Fruit Jar that I'd take the subway into town, and he drove me over near Queens Plaza. I had him pull up there in the shadows of the elevated, and I said. "I'm sorry as hell, Fruit Jar. Will you accept an apology?" And he was feeling good, so he stuck out his hand and said, "Sure, kid. Long as you put it that way, I—"

I jammed his right hand between my knees. I gripped the fingers of his left hand, bending them back, and I snapped the knife open.

"J-Jesus—" His eyes got wider and wider, and his mouth hung open like the mouth of a sack, and the slobber ran down his chin, thick and shiny. "W-whatcha d-doin'...whatcha... aaahhhhh..."

I gave it to him in the neck. I damned near carved his Adam's apple out. I took the big silk handkerchief out of his breast pocket, wiped my hands and the knife, and put the knife in his pocket. (That would give them something to think about.) Then I shoved him down on the floor of the car, and caught the train into town.

And I hadn't ridden to the next station before I saw what a fool I'd been.

Fruit Jar... He could have told me. I could have made him tell me — the thing that might mean the difference between my living and dying. And now he couldn't tell me.

His brother... HIS BROTHER HELL! I almost yelled it out; I think I did say it. But I was up in the front of the car by myself, and no one noticed. People hardly ever notice me. And maybe that's the reason I'm...

His brother... Detroit, 1942... not sure of the details... Not sure! The Man wasn't sure! Christ Almighty. As if he'd have hauled Fruit Jar into this deal without knowing every damned last thing there was to know about him!

He'd hauled him in. Fruit Jar had been sitting pretty with no heat on him and a swell income, and The Man had hauled him in on something that could be very hot. He couldn't say no to The Man. He couldn't even let on that he didn't like it. But he didn't like it; he was sore as hell. And since he couldn't take it out on The Man, he'd taken it out on me.

That was the trouble. Just what I'd thought it was all along. It must have been that... I guessed.

His brother. Even if he'd had a brother, even if he'd had fifty-five brothers and I'd killed them all, he wouldn't have done anything about it. Not, anyway, until after I'd done my job. I should have known that. I did know it when I stopped to think.

Jim Thompson

But The Man had shot me the line fast, and I wasn't thinking. Why think when it's so easy to kill?

The Man wanted me to believe that Fruit Jar had come down to Peardale that day on his own. He had to make me think that, or I'd think of another reason for Fruit Jar being there...the real reason. Because he'd been sent. It might blow the job if I knew that. I might blow it and get away...instead of getting what a guy always got for blowing or running out.

Fruit Jar wasn't very bright. He hadn't needed to be very bright for the job The Man had sent him to do—to deliver some dough, maybe, or maybe to throw in a good chill as the clincher to a deal. But he hadn't been even that bright. He'd missed connections somehow with the party he was supposed to see, and instead of beating it and trying again later he'd screwed around waiting. He'd gone out of his way to needle me.

I'd scratched him up with the knife, and he'd been a little worried when he took off for the city. He had a pretty good idea that he'd pulled a boner. And he should have known what The Man was like—when The Man was really sore at you, you never knew it—but he wasn't bright, like I've said, and...

Or was it that way? Was I knocking myself out over nothing? Had The Man given me the straight dope?

He might have. A guy like me—well, he gets so used to looking around corners that he can't see in a straight line. The more true a thing is, the less he can believe it. The Man could have leveled with me. I was damned sure he hadn't, but he could have. He had—*he hadn't*. He hadn't—*he had*.

94

I didn't know. I couldn't be sure. And it wasn't The Man's fault and it wasn't Fruit Jar's. There was just one guy to blame, a stupid, dried-up jerk named Charles Bigger.

Big shot... Bright boy...

I could feel it. The hard glaze spreading over my eyes. I could feel my heart pounding—pounding like someone pounding on a door. Pounding like a scared kid locked in a closet. I could feel my lungs drawing up like fists, tight and hard and bloodless, forcing the blood up into my brain.

There was a crowd of people waiting to get on the train at Times Square. I went through them. I walked right through them. Giving it to them in the ribs and insteps. And no one said anything, so maybe they sensed what was in me and knew they were lucky. Because they were lucky.

There was a woman getting on, and I gave it to her in the breasts with my elbow, so hard she almost dropped the baby she was carrying. And she was lucky, too, but maybe the baby wasn't. Maybe it would have been better off down under the wheels. Everything ended.

Why not? Tell me why not.

I walked back to Forty-seventh Street, and somewhere along the way I bought a couple of newspapers. I rolled them up tight under my arm, and their hardness felt good to me. I rolled them tighter, and slapped them against the palm of my hand. And that felt good, too. I walked along, swinging them against my hand, swinging them like a club, the motions getting shorter and shorter, jerkier and jerkier, and...

"Temper, temper—"

Who was it that'd said that?...I grinned and it made my mouth hurt, and the hurt felt good... *"Temper, temper—"*

Sure. I knew. Have to watch the temper-temper. So I'd watch it. I liked to watch it. There was only one thing I'd like better... but everyone saw how lucky they were. And in a minute or two I'd be alone in my room. And it would be all right then.

I walked up the two flights of stairs. There was only one elevator and it was crowded, and I had enough sense to know that I'd better not get on it.

I climbed the stairs to the third floor, and walked down the corridor to the last room on the right. And I leaned against it a moment, panting and shaking. I leaned there, quivering like I'd been through a battle, and...

And I heard it. Heard the splashing and humming.

The quivering and the panting stopped. I turned the door knob. It was unlocked.

I stood in the doorway of the bathroom looking at her.

She was scooted down in the tub of suds, one arm raised up so she could soap it under the pit. She saw me, and she dropped the washcloth and let out a little squeal.

"C-carl, honey! You scared me to death."

"What are you doing here?" I said.

"Why"—she tilted her head to one side, smiling at me lazily—"you don't recognize Mrs. Jack Smith?"

"What are you doing here?"

"Don't speak to me that way, Carl! After all—"

"What are you doing here?"

The smile began to shrink, pull in around the edges. "Don't be mad, honey. I — I — don't look at me like that. I know I was supposed to come in tomorrow, but —"

"Get out of there," I said.

"But you don't understand, honey! You see, sis and her boy friend drove out to Peardale, a-and I — it was perfectly n-natural for me to r-ride back to the city with them — No one could think there was anything w-wrong with —"

I didn't hear what she said. I didn't want to. I heard but I made myself not hear. I didn't want any explanations. I didn't want it to be all right. I was scared sick, so damned sick, and I was already sliding into Fruit Jar's shoes. And I couldn't pull back, I couldn't run. They were all watching and waiting, looking for the chance to trip me up.

All I could do was kill.

"Get out of there," I said.

I was slapping the newspapers into my palm. *"Get — slap — out — slap — of there — slap, slap, Get — slap . . ."*

Her face was as white as the suds, but she had guts. She forced the smile back, tilted her head again. "Now, honey. With you standing there? Why don't you go on and get in bed, and I'll —"

"Get — slap — out — slap — of there — slap, slap . . ."

"P-please, honey. I'm s-sorry if — I'll be sweet to you, honey. It's been more than a year, and h-honey you don't know — Y-you don't know how s-sweet — all the things I'll —"

She stopped talking. I had my hand knotted in her hair, and I was pulling her up out of the water. And she didn't try to pull

97

away. She came up slowly, her neck, her breasts, the soapsuds sliding away from them like they didn't want to let go.

She stood up.

She stepped out of the tub.

She stood there on the bathmat, fighting with everything she had to fight with—offering it all to me. And she saw it wasn't enough. She knew it before I knew it myself.

She raised her arms very slowly—so slowly that they hardly seemed to move—and wrapped them around her head.

She whispered, "N-not in the face, Carl. J-just don't hit me in the—"

I flicked the newspapers across her stomach. Lightly. I flicked them across her breasts. I drew them back over my shoulder and—and held them there. Giving her a chance to yell or try to duck. Hoping she'd try it... and stop being lucky.

There were too many lucky people in the world.

"You're a pretty good actress," I said. "Tell me you're not an actress. Tell me you haven't been leading me on, acting hard-boiled and easy-to-get so you could screw me up. Go on, tell me. Call me a liar."

She didn't say anything. She didn't even move.

I let the newspapers drop from my hand. I stumbled forward, and sat down on the toilet stool, and made myself start laughing. I whooped with laughter, I whooped and choked and sputtered, rocking back and forth on the stool. And it was as though a river were washing through me, washing away all the fear and craziness and worry. Leaving me clean and warm and relaxed.

It had always been that way. Once I could start laughing I was all right.

Then, I heard her snicker, and a moment later that husky saloon-at-midnight laugh. And she hunkered down in front of me, laughing, burying her head in my lap.

"Y-you crazy tough little bastard, you! You've taken ten years off my life."

"So now you're sixteen," I said. "I'm going to count on it."

"Crazy! What in the name of God got into you, anyway?" She raised her head, laughing, but looking a little worried. "It was all right to come in, wasn't it, as long as sis and—"

"Sure, it was all right," I said. "It was swell. I'm tickled to death you're here. I've just had a hell of a hard day and I wasn't expecting you, and—Let it go at that. Let me up off this toilet before I fall in."

"Yeah, but, honey—"

I tilted her chin up with my fist. "Yeah? We leave it at that or not?"

"Well—" She hesitated; and then she nodded quickly and jumped up. "Stinker! Toughie! Come on and I'll give you a drink."

She had a pint of whiskey in her overnight bag. She opened it after she'd slipped into her nightgown, and we sat cross-legged on the bed together, drinking and smoking and talking. There weren't many preliminaries to go through. I'd broken the ice but good there in the bathroom. She knew who I was now, if she hadn't had a damned good idea before. She knew why I was in Peardale. She knew why I'd had her come into the city. And it was okay with her.

"Little Bigger," she said, her eyes shining at me. "Little Bigger. Why, my God, honey, I've been hearing about you ever—"

"Okay," I said, "so I'm famous. Now just wipe it out of your head, and leave it wiped out."

"Sure, honey. Carl."

"I don't know how I'll do it. We'll have to work that out. Now, about the dough—"

She was smart there. She might have said fifteen or twenty grand. And I might have said yes. And then I might have thought, I might have passed the word along: The dame's hungry; maybe we'd better keep her quiet...

"Aw, honey—" She made a little face. "Let's not talk about it like I was doing it for—for *that*. We'll be together, won't we? Afterwards? And I know you're not the kind to be stingy."

"It'll be a long time afterwards," I said. "I'll have to stay there at least until summer. You can leave any time, of course, but I couldn't get together with you before summer."

"I can wait. Where would we go, honey? I mean after—"

"We'll work it out. That's no problem. You got money, there's always some place to go. Hell, we could live here or anywhere after a couple of years, when things cool off enough."

"You won't...You don't think I'm awful, do you, Carl?"

"How do I know? I haven't had you yet."

"You know what I mean, honey...You won't think I'd—I-d do the same thing to...You won't be afraid of me, honey? You won't think you have to—"

I tamped out my cigarette.

"Listen to me," I said. "Listening? Then get this. If I was afraid of you you wouldn't be here. Know what I mean?"

She nodded. "I know what you mean."

"Carl, honey..." That husky voice; it was like having cream poured over you. "Aren't you—?"

"Aren't I what?"

She gestured toward the light.

10

That next week is hard to tell about. So much happened. So many things that I couldn't understand—or, that I was afraid to understand. So many things that kept me worried and on edge or scared the living hell out of me.

I had time. I knew I had to take time. The Man didn't want the job done for at least ten weeks, so I should have been able to get my bearings and plan and take things kind of easy. But after that first week—hell, before the week was halfway over—I had an idea that what I and The Man wanted didn't make any difference.

This might be the first week, but I had a damned good idea that it wasn't far from the last one.

That was the week that Kendall really began to show his hand...At least, it seemed he was showing it.

That was the week that Jake tried to frame me.

It was the week he tried to kill me.

It was the week Fay and I began brawling.

It was the week Ruthie...

Jesus! Jesus God, that week! Even now—and what do I have to worry about now?—it rips the guts out of me to think about it.

But let's take things in order. Let's go back to the Friday before the week began, to Fay and me at the hotel.

…She's said it had been over a year since you know what, and I kind of think it must have been an understatement.

And, then, finally, she gave me a long good-night kiss, about fifty kisses rolled into one, and turned on her side. And a minute later she began to snore.

It wasn't a real snore, one of the buzzsaw variety. It was as though there was some small obstruction in her nose where the moisture kept gathering and cutting loose in a little *pop-crack* on about every tenth breath.

I lay there, stiff and tense, counting her breaths, wishing by God that it was a faucet, wanting to grab her by the nose and twist it off. I'd lie there counting her breaths, getting set for the little *pop-crack* that stabbed through me like a hot needle. And just when I had the damned thing about timed, she broke the rhythm on me. She started *pop-cracking* on a seven count, then a nine, and finally a twelve.

It went up from there to a point where she was taking twenty breaths before it came, and finally—God, it seemed like about forty-eight hours later!—finally it stopped.

Maybe you've slept with someone like that; tried to sleep. One of those people who can't get into dreamland good unless they're lying all over you. Well, she was that way. And now that she'd got that goddamned *pop-cracking* out of her system, she started in on the other, scrounging around in the bed. It was hell.

I tried to make myself sleep; but it was no dice. I got to thinking about a guy I'd met that time I skipped out of New York. I couldn't sleep, so I began thinking.

I'd been afraid to show myself on a train or bus or plane, so I'd started hitchhiking up toward Connecticut. I planned on getting up near the Canadian border, where I could jump across fast if I had to, and swinging west from there. Well, this guy picked me up, and he had a good car, and I knew he must have dough on him. But... well, it doesn't make sense the way it turned out; *he* didn't make sense, like you ordinarily think of a guy making it. Anyway...

He was a writer, only he didn't call himself that. He called himself a hockey peddler. "You notice that smell?" he said. "I just got through dumping a load of crap in New York, and I ain't had time to get fumigated." All I could smell was the whiz he'd been drinking. He went on talking, not at all grammatical like you might expect a writer to, and he was funny as hell.

He said he had a farm up in Vermont, and all he grew on it was the more interesting portions of the female anatomy. And he never laughed or cracked a smile, and the way he told about it he almost made you believe it. "I fertilize them with wild goat manure," he said. "The goats are tame to begin with, but they soon go wild. The stench, you know. I feed them on the finest grade grain alcohol, and they have their own private cesspool to bathe in. But nothing does any good. You should see them at night when they stand on their heads, howling."

I grinned, wondering why I didn't give it to him. "I didn't know goats howled," I said.

"They do if they're wild enough," he said.

"Is that all you grow?" I said. "You don't have bodies on any of — of those things?"

"Jesus Christ!" He turned on me like I'd called him a dirty name. "Ain't I got things tough enough as it is? Even butts and breasts are becoming a drug on the market. About all there's any demand for any more is you know what." He passed me the bottle, and had a drink himself, and he calmed down a little. "Oh, I used to grow other things," he said. "Bodies. Faces. Eyes. Expressions. Brains. I grew them in a three-dollar-a-week room down on Fourteenth Street and I ate aspirin when I couldn't raise the dough for a hamburger. And every now and then some lordly book publisher would come down and reap my crop and package it at two-fifty a copy, and, lo and behold, if I praised him mightily and never suggested that he was a member of the Jukes family in disguise, he would spend three or four dollars on advertising and the sales of the book would swell to a total of nine hundred copies and he would give me ten per cent of the proceeds...when he got around to it." He spat out the window and took another drink. "How about driving a while?"

I slid over him, over behind the wheel, and his hands slid over me. "Let's see the shiv," he said.

"The what?"

"The pig-sticker, the switchblade, the knife, for Christ's sake. Don't you understand English? You ain't a publisher, are you?"

I gave it to him. I didn't know what the hell else to do. He tested the blade with his thumb. Then he opened the pocket of the car, fumbled around inside and brought out a little whetstone.

"Christ," he said, drawing the blade back and forth across it. "You ought to keep this thing sharp. You can't do any good with a goddamn hoe like this. I'd sooner try to cut a guy's throat with a bed slat... Well"—he handed it back to me—"that's the best I can do. Just don't use it for nothing but belly work and it may be all right."

"Now, look," I said. "What—what—"

"You look," he said. He reached over and took the Luger out of my belt. He held it down under the dashlight and looked at it. "Well, it ain't too bad," he said. "But what you really need is a rod like this." And he reached into the pocket again and took out a .32 Colt automatic. "Like to try it? Come on and try it on me. Stop the car and try them both."

He shoved them at me, reaching for the switch key, and—and, hell, I don't know what I said.

Finally, he laughed—different from the way he'd laughed before, more friendly—and put the Luger back in my belt and the Colt back into the car pocket.

"Just not much sense to it, is there?" he said. "How far you want to ride?"

"As far as I can," I said.

"Swell. That'll be Vermont. We'll have time to talk."

We went straight on through, taking turns about driving and going in places for coffee and sandwiches, and most of the time he was talking or I was. Not about ourselves, nothing personal,

I mean. He wasn't nosy. Just about books and life and religion, and things like that. And everything he said was so kind of off-trail I was sure I could remember it, but somehow later on it all seemed to boil down pretty well to just one thing.

"Sure there's a hell…" I could hear him saying it now, now, as I lay here in bed with her breath in my face, and her body squashed against me… "It is the drab desert where the sun sheds neither warmth nor light and Habit force-feeds senile Desire. It is the place where mortal Want dwells with immortal Necessity, and the night becomes hideous with the groans of one and the ecstatic shrieks of the other. Yes, there is a hell, my boy, and you do not have to dig for it…"

When I finally left him, he gave me a hundred and ninety-three dollars, everything he had in his wallet except a ten-spot. And I never saw him again, I don't even know his name.

Fay started snoring again.

I got the whiskey bottle and my cigarettes, and went into the bathroom. I closed the door, and sat down on the stool. And I must have sat there two or three hours, smoking and sipping whiskey and thinking.

I wondered what had ever happened to that guy, whether he was still in Vermont growing those things. I think about what he'd said about hell, and it had never meant more to me than it did right now.

I wasn't an old man by a hell of a long ways, but I got to wondering whether the way I felt had anything to do with getting older. And that led into wondering how old I really was, anyway, because I didn't know.

About all I had to go on was what my mother told me, and she'd told me one thing one time, and another thing another time. I doubt that she really knew, offhand. She might have figured it out, but with all the kids she'd had she didn't get much figuring done. So...

I tried to dope it out, a screwy thing like that. I added up and subtracted and tried to remember back to certain times and places, and all I got out of it was a headache.

I'd always been small. Except for those few years in Arizona, it seemed like I'd always been living on the ragged edge.

I thought way back, and if things had ever been very much different or I'd ever been very much different, I couldn't remember when it was.

I sipped and smoked and thought, and finally I caught myself nodding:

I went back into the bedroom.

She was sleeping in a kind of loose ball, now, with her rear end way over on one side of the bed and her knees on the other. That left some space at the foot of the bed, so I lay down across that.

I woke up with her feet on my chest, feeling like my ribs had been caved in. It was nine o'clock. I'd had less than four hours' sleep. But I knew I wasn't going to get any more, so I slid out from under her and got up.

I went to the toilet and took a bath, being as quiet about it as I could. I was standing in front of the bathroom mirror, fitting the contact lenses into place, when I saw her looking in the doorway.

She didn't know that I saw her. It's funny how people will watch you in a mirror without thinking that you're bound to be watching them. She was looking at the lower part of my face, my mouth, and I saw her grimace. Then, she caught herself, catching on to the fact, I guess, that I might be able to see her. She moved back into the bedroom, waited a moment, and headed for the door again, making enough noise for me to know that she was up.

I slipped my teeth into place. I guess my mouth did look bad without them—kind of like it belonged in another location. But I didn't give a damn whether she liked it or not.

She came in yawning, drowsily scratching her head with both hands. "Gosh, honey," she said. "What'd you get up so early for? I was sleeping sooo-ahh—'scuse me—so good."

"It's after nine," I said. "I figured I'd been in bed long enough."

"Well, I hadn't. You woke me up with all your banging around."

"Maybe I'd better go stand in the corner."

Her eyes flashed. Then she laughed, half irritably. "Grouchy. You don't have to snap me up on everything. Now, get out of here and let me take a bath."

I got out, and let her. I dressed while she bathed and started brushing her teeth—washing her mouth out a thousand and fifty times, it sounded like, gargling and spitting and hacking. I began getting sick at my stomach; rather, I got sicker than I already was. I threw down the rest of the whiskey fast, and that helped. I picked up the phone and ordered breakfast and another pint. And I knew how bad the whiz was for me—I'd been told not to drink it at all—but I have to have it.

She was still horsing around in the bathroom when the waiter came. I got down another fast drink; then, I gulped and coughed and a whole mouthful of blood came up in my handkerchief.

I raised the bottle again. I lowered it, holding my breath, swallowing as rapidly as I could. And there wasn't any blood that time—none came up—but I knew it was there.

I'd already been damned sick in front of her once. If I was sick very much; if she thought I might be on the way down... down like Jake...

11

She came out of the bathroom feeling a lot better than when she went in, and with a fresh half pint of whiskey in me I wasn't feeling so bad myself. We ate all the breakfast, with her helping out quite a bit on my share. I lighted cigarettes for us, and she lay back on the pillows.

"Well?" she crinkled her eyes at me.

"Well, what?" I said.

"How was it?"

"Best coffee I ever drank," I said.

"Stinker!" She let out with that guffaw again. I was getting to where I waited for that, too, like I'd waited for her snoring. "Mmm?" she said. "I do if you do. Want to come back to bed with mama?"

"Look, baby," I said. "I'm sorry as hell, but—well, you'll have to be starting back."

"Huh!" She sat up. "Aw, now, honey! You said—"

"I said we'd stay overnight. We've done it. It doesn't make any difference whether—"

"It does too make a difference! You haven't been stuck in that

111

God-forsaken hole as long as I have! I... Why don't we do it like we planned, honey? I can go back tonight, and you can come tomorrow... that'll give us a whole day together. Or I can stay—I'll go over and stay with sis tonight—and come tomorrow, and you can—"

"Look, baby; look, Fay," I said. "I guess I hadn't thought the thing through. I've had plenty of things to think about, and I couldn't see that it mattered much whether—"

"Of course, it matters! Why wouldn't it matter?"

"You've got to go back," I said. "Now. Or I'll start back and you can come later on in the day. I can't stay at the house overnight unless you're there. I've got to have you there to yes me, in case something pops with Jake. If he should get out of line like he did the first night—"

"Pooh! For all we know he may not even come home."

"That's another thing. He's got to start staying there. All the time. You'll have to see that he does. He can't just be there on the one night that something happens to him."

"Hell!" She stamped out her cigarette angrily, and reached for the bottle. "Just when I think I'm going to... Well, gosh, honey. You could go back tomorrow, and I could go back tonight. Why wouldn't that be all right?"

"I'm afraid of it. I'm not supposed to have much dough. It doesn't look right for me to take damned near three days to pick up a suit."

She slammed the whiskey bottle down angrily.

"I'm sorry as hell, Fay," I said.

She didn't say anything.

"We just can't take chances now. We've got too much to

lose—" I went on talking and explaining and apologizing; and I knew she'd better snap out of it fast or she wouldn't be able to get back to Peardale.

Finally, she turned back around; maybe she noticed the tightening of my voice. "All right, honey," she sighed, half pouting. "If that's the way it is, why that's the way it is."

"Fine. That's my baby," I said. "We'll have our good times. Just you and me and thirty grand; maybe five or ten more if it's an A-1 job."

"Oh, I know, Carl," her smile was back. "It'll be wonderful. And I'm awfully sorry if I—I was just kind of disappointed and—"

"That's okay," I said.

She wanted me to go back to Peardale first. She wanted to laze around a while, and take her time about dressing. I said it would be all right. Just so she showed before night.

We chewed the fat a while longer; just talking without saying much. After a while, she said, "Mmmmm, honey?" and held out her arms to me; and I knew I couldn't do it. Not so soon, not now. God, Jesus, I knew I couldn't do it.

But I did!

I struggled and strained, aching clear down to my toenails; and I kept my eyes closed, afraid to let her see what she might see in them, and... *and I was in that drab desert where the sun shed neither heat nor light, and...*

...What about that afterwards, anyway? If there was an afterwards. What about her?

I stared out the dirty window of the Long Island train, half dozing, my mind wandering around and around and drifting back to her. What about her?

She was stacked. She was pretty. She was just about everything you could want in a woman—as long as you were on top or you looked like you might be on top.

But I couldn't see it, the one big long party which was what it would be like with her. I couldn't see it, and couldn't take it. What I wanted was...well, I wasn't sure but it wasn't that. Just to be by myself. Maybe with someone like—well, like Ruthie—someone I could be myself around.

Ruth. Fay. Fay, Ruth. Or what? I didn't know what I wanted. I wasn't even real sure about what I didn't want. I hadn't wanted to be dragged in on this mess, but I had to admit I'd been getting pretty fed up out there in Arizona. I'd kept quiet about it, but I'd had more than one babe in my shack. Hell, the last month, I'd had two or three a week, a different one each time. And they were all okay, I guess, they all had plenty on the ball. But somehow none of them seemed to be it—whatever it was I wanted.

Whatever it was I wanted.

My eyes drifted shut, and stayed shut. The Man would probably have something to say about Fay. He might see a spot where he could use her again, or he might decide that she was a bad risk. He'd talk to me about it, of course. And if I wanted her, and was responsible for her...

I didn't know. I didn't want her now, her or anyone else. But that was natural enough. Tomorrow, the next day...afterwards? I didn't know.

My head fell over against the window, and I went to sleep.

It was hours later when I woke up.

I was way the hell out to the end of the line, and the conductor was shaking me.

Somehow I managed to keep from punching the stupid bastard in the face. I paid the extra fare, plus the fare back to Peardale. It was still early afternoon. I could still get back to Peardale well ahead of her.

I went to the john and washed my face. I came back to my seat, studying the minute hand on my watch, wondering what the hell was holding us up. And then I glanced out the window, and started cursing.

Mr. Stupid, the conductor, who should have picked up my seat check and put me off at Peardale—he and all the other trainmen were sauntering up the street together. Taking their own sweet time about it. Shoving and grab-assing with each other, and braying like a bunch of mules.

They turned in at a restaurant.

They stayed in there, doing what God only knows, because they couldn't have been eating that long. They must have stayed in the place two hours.

Finally, when I was just about ready to go up into the locomotive and drive off by myself, they got through doing whatever they were doing and sauntered back to the station again. They got there, eventually, back to the station. But, of course, they didn't climb on the damned train and get going.

They had to stand around on the station platform, gabbing and picking their teeth.

I cursed them to myself, calling them every dirty name I could think of. They were trying to screw me up.

They broke it up at last, and began climbing on the train.

It was dark when we got into Peardale. A train from the city was just pulling out. I looked through the station door and saw a taxi on the other side — the only taxi there.

He swung the door open, and I climbed in. And — but I guess I don't need to tell you. I'd tried to be so damned careful, yet here she was, here we were, riding home together.

She gave me a startled, half-scared look. I said, "Why, hello, Mrs. Winroy. Just come out from New York?"

"Y-yes." She bobbed her head. "Did — did you?"

I laughed. It sounded as hollow as that conductor's head. "Not exactly. I left the city this morning but I fell asleep on the train. They carried me out to the end of the line, and I'm just now getting back."

"Well," she said. Just well. But the way she said it, she was saying a whole lot more.

"I was all worn out," I said. "A friend I stayed with in New York snored all night, and I didn't get much sleep."

She turned her head sharply, glaring at me. Then she bit her lip, and I heard a sound that was halfway between a snicker and a snort.

We reached the house. She went on inside, and I paid off the driver and went across the street to the bar.

I drank two double shots. Then I ordered a ham and cheese sandwich and a bottle of ale, and sat down in one of the booths. I was easing down a little. It was a stupid mixup, but it was just one, and it would be hard for anyone to make anything out of it. Anyway, it was done, and there wasn't any use worrying.

I ordered another ale, easing my nerves down, arguing away the worry. I almost convinced myself that it had been a good break. It could be, if you looked at it in the right way. Because any damned fool ought to know that we wouldn't be goofy enough to lay up in town, and then ride home together.

I finished the ale, started to order a third one, and decided against it. I'd had enough. More than enough. Or I never would have. You take just so much from the bottle, and then you stop taking. From then on you're putting.

I picked up my suit box and crossed the street to the house. Half hoping that Jake was on hand.

He was.

He and Fay and Kendall were all in the living room together, and she was laughing and talking a mile a minute.

I went in, giving them a nod and a hello as I headed for the stairs. Fay turned and called to me.

"Come in, Mr. Bigelow. I was just telling about your train ride—how you went to sleep and rode to the end of the line. What did you think when you woke up?"

"I thought I'd better start carrying an alarm clock," I said.

Kendall chuckled. "That reminds me of an occasion several years ago when—"

"Excuse me"—Fay cut in on him—"Jake—"

He was bent forward in his chair, staring at the floor, his big bony hands folded across each other.

117

Jim Thompson

"Jake...Just a moment, Mr. Bigelow. My husband wants to apologize to you."

"That's not necessary," I said. "I—"

"I know. But he wants to...don't you, Jake? He knows he made a very foolish mistake, and he wants to apologize for it."

"That's right," Kendall nodded primly. "I'm sure Mr. Winroy is anxious to rectify any misunderstandings which—uh—can be rectified."

Jake's head came up suddenly, "Oh, yeah?" he snarled. "Who pulled your chain, grandpa?"

Kendall looked down into the bowl of his pipe. "Your grand-parent?" he said, musingly. "I believe that is just about the foulest name anyone ever called me."

Jake blinked stupidly. Then it registered on him, and he dragged the back of his hand across his mouth like he'd been slapped. All the fight in him, the little he had left, went away again. He looked from Kendall to Fay and then, finally, at me. And I guess mine was about the friendliest face there.

He got up and sagged toward me, a big drained-empty sack of guts. He came toward me, holding out his hand, trying to work up a smile, the sly, sick look of a beaten dog on his face.

And I couldn't help feeling sorry for him, but the flesh crawled on the back of my neck. He'd had too much. He was too beaten. When they get that far gone, you'd better get in the final licks fast.

"S-sorry, lad. Musta had one too many. No hard feelings?" I said it was okay, but he didn't hear me. He clung to my hand, turning to look at Fay. He stared, frowned puzzledly, then

118

turned back to me again. "Glad to have you here. Anything I can do I — I — I —"

That was as much of his speech as he could remember. He dropped my hand, and looked at her again. She nodded briskly, took him by the arm, and led him out of the room.

They went out to the porch, and the door didn't quite close; and I heard her say, "Now, you'd better not disappoint me, Jake. I've had just about —"

Kendall pushed himself up out of his chair. "Well, Mr. Bigelow. You look rather tired if I may say so."

"I am," I said. "I think I'll turn in."

"Excellent. I was just about to suggest it. Can't have you getting sick at a time like this, can we?"

"At a time like this," I said. "How do you mean?"

"Why" — his eyebrows went up a trifle — "just when you're on the threshold of a new life. Your schooling and all. I feel that great things are in store for you here if you can just keep your original objective in mind, keep forging ahead toward it despite divertissements of the moment."

"That's the secret of your success, huh?" I said.

And he colored a little but he smiled, eyes twinkling. "That, I believe, is what might be called leaving one's self wide open. The obvious retort — if I cared to stoop to it — would be an inquiry as to the secret of *your* success."

We said good night, and he went back to the bakery. I started up the stairs.

Fay had seen Jake off for town or wherever he was going, and was out in the kitchen with Ruth. I stood at the foot of the stairs a moment, listening to her lay down the law in that husky, what-are-you-waiting-on voice. Then I cleared my throat loudly, and went on up to my room.

About five minutes later, Fay came in.

She said there wasn't a thing to worry about. Kendall and Jake had swallowed the story whole.

"And I'd know if they hadn't, honey. I was watching, believe you me. They didn't suspect a thing."

She was feeling pretty proud of herself. I told her she'd done swell. "Where's Jake gone?"

"To the liquor store. He's going to get a fifth of wine, and he'll probably pick up a couple of drinks in a bar. He damned sure won't get any more than that. I got all his money away from him but two dollars."

"Swell," I said. "That's my baby."

"Mmmmm? Even if I do snore?"

"Ahhh, I was kidding. I was sore about that goddamned train ride."

"We-el, just so you're sorry—" She leaned against me.

I gave her a poke and a kiss, and pushed her away. "Better beat it, now, baby."

"I know. I'm just as anxious to be careful as you are, honey." She reached for the doorknob, then she clapped her hand over her mouth suddenly, stifling a giggle. "Oh, Carl! There's something I just have to tell you."

"Yeah?" I said. "Don't take too long about it."

"You'll die laughing. I don't know why I didn't see it before, but she's just not the kind of person you pay much attention to and—And of course it may have just happened. I—You just won't believe it, honey! It's just so—"

"That is funny," I said. "Better not tell me any more or I'll be laughing all night."

"Stinker! Just for that…It's Ruthie, honey. Would you believe it? I swear to God someone's gotten to her."

12

I laughed. I did a pretty good job of it, considering. "No fooling. How did she happen to tell you about it?"

"She didn't, silly. You can see it. It sticks out all over her."

"That should be something to see," I said.

"Crazy!" She buried her head against my chest, giggling. "B-but—but, honestly, Carl! Who in the world would want to... Carl! I bet I know."

"Yeah?" I said. "I mean, you do?"

"Why, of course. It couldn't be anyone else. She went home last night. I'll bet it's someone in her own family."

I swallowed. I was relieved, in a way, but I wished she hadn't said it. I felt shamed, embarrassed.

"They're... they're that kind of people?"

"They're trash. You ought to see how they live! They've got about fourteen kids, and—"

"Maybe I ought to tell you," I said. "There were fourteen children in my family."

"Oh—" She hesitated, uncomfortably. "Well. Of course, I didn't mean that—that—"

"Sure. Forget it," I said.

"But it isn't the same, Carl. You didn't just put up with it like they do. You did something about it."

"Well," I said. "Isn't she doing something?"

"Oh, pooh! What good will it do her if she does manage to squeeze through college? Who's going to give *her* a job that's worth having?"

I shook my head. Ruthie looked pretty good to me, but she'd just about have to. She was me, in a way, and I was seeing myself in her.

"...you know I'm right, Carl. She's trash, stupid, like all the rest of her family. If she really had any brains or guts, she'd—she'd—Well, she'd do *something!*"

"Well, maybe she's working on it now. Maybe she's going to grow herself a gang of kids and put them all out to picking cotton."

"All right," she laughed good-naturedly. "I guess my own family didn't amount to much, for that matter, but I did *do*—"

"You'd better start doing something else," I said, "before someone catches you in here."

She kissed me, patted me quickly on the cheek and slipped out of the room.

I went to bed.

It was only a little after nine when I turned in, and I couldn't have slept better if I hadn't had a worry in the world. I woke at six with nine good hours under my belt, the best night's sleep I'd had since I left Arizona. I had a hangover, but nothing bad. I coughed and spit blood, but nothing bad. That rest had done me a world of good.

Well, anyway, I'd had that much.

I smoked a couple of cigarettes, wondering what I'd better do. Whether I'd better get up and get out on the town—stay away from the house until the others were up. Or whether I should just stay here in my room until they were up.

It would have to be one way or another. Otherwise, unless I missed my guess, I'd have Ruthie on my neck. And all Ruthie was getting from me, from now on, was the cold shoulder. I wasn't going to get caught alone with her. Any time I saw her, there'd be someone else around. Pretty soon she'd get the idea, and then maybe it would be safe to be friendly with her... just friendly.

...I found a little lunchroom open down near the railroad station and got some coffee. Afterwards, I sauntered back up the street.

It was Sunday—somehow that fact kept slipping in and out of my mind. You know how that is, maybe, when a lot's been happening to you, and you lay off on days you're used to work-ing and so on. The church bells were starting to ring, booming out over the town. Practically every business house was closed; nothing was open but a few cigar stands, lunch counters and the like. I began to feel kind of conspicuous.

I stopped at an intersection to let a car go past. But instead of passing it pulled even with me and stopped.

Sheriff Summers rolled the window down and leaned out.

"Hey, there, young feller. Give you a lift?"

He was all duked out in a hard-boiled collar and a blue serge suit. There was a hatchet-faced dame with him—a dame in a stiff black satin dress and a hat that looked like a lamp shade. I took off my hat and smiled at her, wondering why some dairy hadn't snapped her up to sour their cream for them.

"What about the lift?" he said, shaking hands. " 'Spect you're headin' for church, eh? Glad to take you t' any one you say."

"Well," I hesitated. "As a matter of fact, I'm not a—I've never affiliated—"

"Just lookin' around, huh? Well, come on and go with us."

I went around to the other side, and he started to open the front door. I opened the back door, and climbed in…How dumb can you be anyway? How little can you know about women? Muss 'em up when they've got their clothes off, that's my motto. When they're dressed up—maybe in the only good thing they've got—give them room.

He drove on. I cleared my throat. "I don't believe I've met your—is it your daughter, sheriff?"

"Huh?" He looked up into the rear-view mirror, startled. Then, he gave her a poke in the ribs with his elbow. "You hear that, Bessie? He thinks you're my daughter."

"And who am I, pray tell?"

"Why—uh—my wife."

"Thank you. I was afraid you'd forgotten."

She half turned in the seat, brushing at the place where he'd poked her, and the way she looked then she wouldn't have stood a chance at that milk-souring job.

"Thank you for the compliment, young man. It's about the

first one I've had since Bill came home from the war. World War One, that is."

"Aw, now, Bessie. I ain't that—"

"Be quiet. Mr. Bigelow and I are thoroughly disgusted with you, aren't we, Mr. Bigelow? There is nothing he can say that we care to hear."

"Not a thing," I grinned. "That's an awfully pretty hat you're wearing, Mrs. Summers."

"Do you hear that, Your Highness? Did you hear what this *gentleman* said about my hat?"

"Well, heck, Bessie. It does look kinda of like a lamp—"

"Hush. Just be quiet, and Mr. Bigelow and I will try to ignore you."

They kept it up all the way to church, and practically up to the door. And they seemed to enjoy it in a way, but I wondered if they wouldn't have enjoyed some other way better. I mean, arguing is arguing, and quarreling is quarreling, and it's still that regardless of how you laugh and kid around about it. You don't do it unless something is eating on you. You don't do it when things are like they should be.

I opened the car door for her and helped her out...and she looked at him. I took her elbow and helped her up the steps of the church...and she looked at him. I stood aside at the door and let her go in first...and she looked at him.

We stayed through Sunday school and church, and you probably know a lot more about those things than I do, so I won't describe them to you. It was better than wandering around the street. It was as good a way as any of killing the morning. I felt safe and peaceful, like a guy has to feel if his brain is going to work at its best. I sang and prayed and listened to the sermon— just sort of letting my mind wander. Letting it go where it wanted to. And by the time church was over, I had it. I'd figured out how I was going to kill Jake Winroy.

Not completely, you understand. There were a few details to iron out, my alibi and setting him up and so on. But I knew they'd come to me.

Mrs. Summers glanced at me as we went back up the aisle together. "Well, young man. You're looking very happy."

"I'm glad you let me come with you," I said. "It's done me a lot of good."

They stopped at the door to shake hands with the minister, and she introduced me. I told him his sermon had been very inspiring...which it was. I'd doped out the plan for Jake while he was spieling.

We started on out to the car, she and I walking together and the sheriff trailing along behind.

"I was wondering, Mr. Big—Oh, I think I'll call you, Carl. If you don't mind."

"I wish you would," I said. "What were you wondering, Mrs. Summers?"

"I was going to ask you if—" We'd reached the curb, and she turned and motioned impatiently. "Oh, do come on, Bill. You're slower than molasses in January. I was about to ask Carl to come home to dinner with us."

"Yeah?" he said. "How come? I mean — uh — you were?"

Her mouth tightened. Untightened. I think she was just about to open up on him when he headed her off.

"Well, fine, great!" He clapped me on the back. "Tickled to death to have you, son. Meant to ask you myself."

He hadn't meant to. He didn't even halfway like the idea. He could take me to church, sure. But to take me into his home — pal up with me — when there was any kind of a chance that I might mean trouble...

There *was* something about me that bothered him. There was something he wasn't quite satisfied about.

"Thanks very much," I said. "I don't think I'd better today. They're expecting me at the house, and I've got a lot of things to get ready for school and — and all."

"Uh-huh. Sure," he nodded. "Well, if you can't make it, you can't...guess we'll have to eat by ourselves, Bessie."

"You," she said. "I'll swear, Bill Summers, I — I —!"

"Now, what'd I do? I asked him, didn't I? You heard him say he couldn't come. Didn't I" — he turned to me — "Didn't you say you couldn't come?"

"Hush. You're impossible. Utterly impossible...Carl, I'd ask you to let us drive you home, but I imagine His Highness would find some way to keep you from accepting."

"Now, I wouldn't neither! Heck, I — why'd I do a thing like that?"

"Why do you do anything, pray tell?"

It was getting embarrassing. I put a stop to it. I said I honestly couldn't take dinner with them today—maybe some other time—but I would appreciate a ride home.

Neither of them said anything until we reached the house. Then, while I was thanking them and saying good morning, he squinted at the coupe pulled in at the gutter.

"Hey," he frowned, "that's Doc Dodson's car, ain't it? You got some sick folks here, son?"

"Not that I know of," I said. "I left the house before anyone was up this morning."

"Must be someone sick. Doc wouldn't be payin' no social calls on the Winroys. Wonder who it could be?"

"Why don't you go in and ask?" Mrs. Summers glared at him. "Shake hands with all of them. Call them all by their first names. Ask about their families. Never mind about *me,* or how *I*—"

He jammed the car into gear, cutting her off. "I'm goin', ain't I? Doggone it, can't you see I'm goin'?...son, I'm—I—"

I hopped out fast. He drove off, the engine roaring, and I went up the walk and into the house.

Fay met me in the hall. She was breathless. The reddish-brown eyes blazed with fear against the dead white of her face. I looked past her, into the dining room.

Ruth was in there. Ruth and Kendall and Jake and a potbellied, bald-headed little guy I knew was a doctor. Jake was sprawled on the floor on his back, and the doctor was stooped down over him, holding a stethoscope to his chest.

Fay whispered to me, her lips barely moving.

"His wine. Poisoned. Doped. Did you—?"

13

I pushed past her, flipping my fist against her groin. Goddammit, of course she was scared, but she didn't need to hang a sign on me. She followed me into the dining room and stood beside me. I moved away from her, over between Kendall and Ruth.

Jake's eyes were closed. He was mumbling, rolling his head from side to side. The doc leaned back, letting the stethoscope swing free, and frowned down at him.

He picked up Jake's wrist and felt the pulse. He let the hand drop back to the floor.

"Hold still," he said curtly.

"... Slee-py... s-so—" Jake kept on rolling his head, breathing in great shuddering breaths "... S-save me... l-lookit... w-wine—"

"Stop that! Stop it this minute!" The doctor gripped him by the head with one hand. "Hold still!"

Jake held still. He had to. The way the doc was gripping him, he might have got his scalp peeled off.

The doctor pulled back first one eyelid, then, the other. He stood up, brushing at the knees of his pants, and nodded to Kendall.

"You tell me how this happened, Phil?"

"Why, yes, Doc." Kendall took the pipe out of his mouth. "I don't know as I can add anything to what Mrs. Winroy—"

"Mrs. Winroy was somewhat excited. You tell me."

"Well, let's see. She and I—Mrs. Winroy and I—were in the living room, reading the Sunday papers, and Miss Dorne was in the kitchen preparing dinner. Isn't that right, Ruth?"

"Y-yes, sir."

"Never mind all that. Just the essentials." The doctor glanced impatiently at his watch. "I can't spend all morning on—on— You heard Winroy coming down the stairs, making plenty of noise about it. Go on."

"I got up. We both got up, I believe. We supposed that— uh—he was just—"

"Drunk. Go on."

"We went out into the hall and he staggered past us, mumbling that he'd been doped—that the wine had been doped, or something of the kind. His speech was very unclear. He came into the dining room and collapsed, and we—Mrs. Winroy—called—"

"He was carrying the wine bottle with him, eh? Very carefully corked?" The doctor's face was flushed; the red seemed to go clear up into his eyes. "Let me see it again."

Kendall took the bottle from the table and handed it to him. He sniffed it, tasted it, took a man-size swallow of it. He brushed his mouth sourly, glancing at Fay.

"He take sleeping pills? How many—how often?"

"I—I don't k-know, doctor."

131

"Know how many he has? Whether any great number is missing?"

"No, I—" Fay shook her head "—I brought him some back from the city, but I don't know how many he had—"

"Did, eh? Have a prescription? No? Know that's illegal? Never mind. No bearing here."

"He's n-not—?"

The doctor grunted. He dug the toe of his shoe into Jake's ribs. "Cut it out. Stop it. Get up from there," he snapped.

Jake's eyes wavered open. "S-something...in the—"

"There's something in it, all right. Alcohol. Twenty percent by volume."

He reached for his medicine kit, nodding grimly at Fay. "Nothing wrong with him. Not a thing in the world. Throw a pail of water on him if he doesn't get up."

"But, I—" Her face was red, too, now. Even redder than his. "Why...I just don't understand—"

"Exhibitionism. Wants attention, sympathy. They hit that stuff long enough they don't make much sense...No, he's not drunk. Hasn't had enough."

Fay grimaced, trying to smile. "I'm terribly sorry, doctor. I'll...if you'll send a bill—"

"I will. And don't call me again, understand? I have sick people to take care of."

He slapped his hat on his head, shook hands with Kendall and slammed out of the house.

Jake sat up. He pushed himself up to his feet, stood weaving, his head sagged, staring at the floor.

"Ruth"—Fay kept her eyes on him—"haven't you some work to do?"

"I—Yes, ma'am." Ruth pivoted on the crutch and scuttled back to the kitchen.

"Jake." Fay moved toward him slowly. "Jake. Look at me!"

"Somethin'...something wrong," he mumbled.

"Oh," she said hoarsely. "Something was wrong, huh? Something wrong. You—you frightened us all half to death—make a big scene here on Sunday—and a-and let me in for a bawling out from that damned snotty Dodson, and—and something's wrong! Is that all you've got to say? Look at me, Jake Winroy!"

He kept his eyes on her feet, mumbling that something was wrong. Moving backward as she came toward him.

He reached the door, and there, as he had that first night, he whirled and made a break for it. I heard him trip and stumble on the steps, but he didn't fall as he had the other time. He got through the gate, and glancing out the window I saw him heading for town at his sagging, loping walk.

Fay turned back toward us. Her lips were trembling, her hands clenching and unclenching. She shrugged—or tried to. She tried to smile. She said, "Well, I g-guess that's t-tha—" Then she sank down into a chair at the table, and buried her head in her arms.

Kendall touched me on the elbow and we went out in the hall together. "Not the most pleasant way to spend the Sabbath, eh? You look like you might be able to use a small libation, Mr. Bigelow."

"I could," I said. "It wouldn't even have to be small."

"So? You will do me the honor, then."

We crossed the street to the bar. There were quite a few people in the place, but the bartender came around from behind the counter fast and showed us to a booth.

He'd never done that for me. I'd never seen him do it for anyone else. Kendall seemed to take it as a matter of course. I wondered about it—this and the way the doctor had kind of kowtowed to him—and I guess I showed it.

"I've lived here the better part of my life, Mr. Bigelow. Or should I say the larger part of it? I grew up with many of these people. I taught school to many."

The bartender brought our drinks, double Scotches. Kendall rocked the ice in his glass, looked up at me slowly. His eyes were twinkling.

"Odd about Winroy, isn't it? Now, he above all people should know that if you *had* been sent here to kill him—*if* you had, Mr. Bigelow—"

"That's not a very pleasant if," I said.

"Sorry. Thoughtless of me. Make it a hypothetical person, then. What good would it do for Winroy to dispose of him? He'd only be postponing the inevitable."

"Yeah?" I said. "I guess I don't know much about those things."

"But it's so elementary! They—his former associates, that is—would be even more determined, if anything. Suppose the officers charged with executing our laws allowed a malefactor to go unpunished, merely because punishment was difficult or dangerous to render him. We'd have chaos, Mr. Bigelow. It simply couldn't be allowed."

I raised my glass and took a drink. "I guess you're right," I said. "It would be that way, wouldn't it? But a mal—a criminal usually does try to get away. He may know it won't do him any good, but he's got to try; he can't just sit."

"Yes. Yes, I suppose so," he nodded. "While there's life there's hope, et cetera. But Winroy—"

"I—I don't know what all this has to do with me," I said. "What you said a moment ago; it sounded like you thought he'd tried to get me in trouble."

"And? Surely you were aware of that."

"Why, no." I shook my head. "I thought it was like the doctor—"

"Tell me, Mr. Bigelow. What do you think the doctor's reaction would have been if there had been a quantity of amytal in the wine? What do you think would have been the end result of the ensuing course of events?"

I stared at him. What did I think? Jesus Christ, I didn't have to think!

He nodded slowly.

"Yes. He tried to—uh—frame you...that's the expression, isn't it? You are here by the grace of God, and, I might say, due to my innate distrust of and dislike for the man. Here, instead of in custody on a charge of attempted murder—or worse."

"But—for God's sake!" I said. "How—?"

"Winroy is not notably an early riser. Neither is he inclined to show consideration to others in the matter of quiet. So, when I heard him moving about early this morning—moving with attempted but not too successful stealth—I was disturbed. I got up and listened at my door. I heard him creep out of his room and enter yours. When he came out and went downstairs, I investigated. I—I hope you don't think it was presumptuous of me to enter your room, but my thought was that he might have harmed—"

"I don't. That's all right," I said. "Just—"

"He was too obvious about it. If he'd used any subtlety at all, but…It was a box of amytal, Mr. Bigelow. He'd emptied six of the capsules and left the empty ones in the box with the full ones. And he'd placed the box behind the window curtain, where anyone who suspected wrongdoing would have no difficulty in finding it. Well, I suspected. I saw what he must intend. I went into his room and examined his wine with a result which you are, of course, aware of. I might have simply called him to account, but it seemed best to thwart him. To make him appear so painfully ridiculous that any future similar attempt would be knocked in the head at the outset… You see that, do you not?"

I saw it. Jake wouldn't pull another stunt like that.

"I disposed of the amytal capsules in the toilet along with the wine. Then, I washed the bottle out, and refilled it to its former level from a bottle I had. I am not what is ordinarily thought of as a drinking man, but a small glass of wine, sometimes, when I am turning through a book—"

"He had to take a drink of it," I said. "He'd want to have at least a little of the amytal in him. It's a wonder he didn't—"

"Notice the taste?" Kendall chuckled, his eyes twinkling. "Well, I don't imagine he's accustomed to drinking amytal and liquor, so he'd hardly know what taste to expect. And I imagine it did taste rather peculiar to him. It's much better wine than he's accustomed to drinking."

I looked down at the table. "Gosh," I said. "I hardly know what to say. Except thanks. I don't like to think what would have happened if—"

"Then don't. And I enjoyed doing it, Mr. Bigelow. I can't remember when I've had such an interesting experience."

"What do you think?" I said. "Do you think I should move out?"

"What do *you* think?"

I hesitated. Was he or wasn't he? If he was tied up with The Man, I'd better not be thinking about moving. But if he wasn't, well, moving would be the first thing I'd think of.

"I've been trying to make up my mind," I said. "I'd hate to. People would naturally wonder about it, and it's reasonable there—the price, I mean. And with us working together and the bakery so nearby, it's—"

"I don't believe I'd move, if I were you."

"Well," I said. "I certainly wouldn't want to."

"I hope you don't. I very much hope so. Of course, I wouldn't want you to let me influence you against your better judgement."

"Sure. I understand."

"I admired you a great deal at your first encounter with Winroy. Your complete self-possession. Your self-control, nerve, in the face of an alarming and awkward situation. Frankly, I was a little envious of you; you shamed me. I had just about arrived at a point where I was ready to move myself. In other words, I was going to allow this drunken lout, a convicted gangster, to dictate to *me*. That would have been wrong of me, Mr. Bigelow. Very wrong. But I needn't tell you that, of course. I can't tell you how disappointed I'd be, if you should — well, it sounds rather harsh but I'll say it. If you should turn tail and run."

"I'm not going to," I said. "I'm going to stay, all right."

"Good. Excellent. We shall stand shoulder to shoulder in this matter. You may depend on my fullest support, moral and otherwise. In case of difficulty, I believe you will find that my word carries far more weight in this community than Winroy's."

"I'm sure it does," I said.

"Well—" He raised his glass. "By the way, am I mistaken or did Sheriff and Mrs. Summers drive you home?"

"I ran into them downtown this morning," I said. "I went to church with them."

"Splendid! Those seemingly small things — they mean a great deal in a town like this...Another drink?"

I shook my head. I wanted one, but I didn't think I'd better take it.

He might get the idea that I needed the stuff to keep going.

We went back to the house, and he and I had dinner together alone. Fay was in her room, I guess, still too upset and sore to eat.

We finished eating, and he went to the bakery. And I went right along with him. We came back at seven for sandwiches and coffee and so on — what they usually feed you for Sunday night supper wherever you are. Then we returned to the bakery, and I stuck with him until he knocked off at ten o'clock.

I was afraid to be there in the house with Ruth when all the others were out of the way. I hoped she got the idea fast that I didn't know her from now on.

Sunday is a big night in a bakery, Kendall explained. On Saturday there's practically nothing to do, since most retail outlets are closed the following day. But on Sunday you're baking for Monday, and with almost everyone run out of stuff over the weekend, it's the busiest day of the week.

He had plenty to do out on the floor, and most of the time I was by myself in the stockroom. I kept busy, as busy as I could. It would have looked funny to loaf around for seven or eight hours. He gave me a set of his whites to wear — we were about the same size — and I went all through the stock, getting familiar with it and taking inventory of everything but the bulk stuff.

"You can inventory that tomorrow," Kendall said, when he dropped in on me during a lull. "You'll need someone to help you weigh it, and give you the tare — the weight of the various containers. That would have to be deducted from your gross weight, understand, to give you the net."

I nodded, and he went on:

"These bulk items, they're the things that have given us trouble. Not at all surprising, either, with everyone chasing in and out of here, tossing their batches together by guess and by golly. Now here" — he tapped a heavily insulated barrel — "is a plaster-of-Paris compound —"

"Plaster of Paris," I said. "You put that stuff in — in —?"

"In bread. A few ounces in a large batch of bread does wonders for the texture, and of course it's completely harmless. A very little more than a few ounces, well, you'd have something resembling paving blocks." He smiled, his eyes gleaming behind the glasses. "Your dough would be wasted unless, say, you cared to pelt our friend Winroy in the head with it."

"I see," I laughed. "Yeah."

At ten o'clock we dressed out together. Quite a few of the other workmen were changing clothes at the same time, but he didn't introduce me, as I kind of thought he should. We started up the stairs to the street. And the locker room had been plenty quiet a moment before, but the minute we left you could hear the talk starting up.

"By the way," he said, as we walked home. "I was very favorably impressed by your industry tonight, Mr. Bigelow. I felt justified in beginning your pay instead of waiting until tomorrow."

"Well, thanks," I said. "Thanks very much, Mr. Kendall."

"Not at all, Mr. Bigelow."

"About"—I hesitated—"about my name, Mr. Kendall. It seems kind of funny for you to be mistering me. Wouldn't you rather call me Carl?"

"Would you prefer that I did?"

"Well, I—it would be all right," I said.

"I'm sure it would. But I think we might well leave things as they are." He paused to knock out his pipe on the gate-post; then we went on up the walk together. "Man is forced to give up so much of his dignity by the mere exigencies of existence. It seems to me that he should cling sturdily to the few shreds that are left to him."

"I see," I said. "I just didn't want you to feel—"

"Moreover, as a somewhat more than casual student of human nature, I believe you resent being called by your first name, at least on short acquaintance. I think our reactions are much the same in that respect."

The house was quiet, dark except for the hall lights. We said good night, whispering, and he went to his room and I went to mine.

I took out my contact lenses. I took out my teeth, and stood in front of the mirror massaging my gums. They ached; they always did. There was something wrong with the jawbones—they were soft and they weren't shaped right. I'd never had a set of teeth that didn't make my mouth hurt. Not too bad, understand. Just a steady nagging ache that chewed away at you a little at a time.

I put the teeth back in, and went to bed.

It was after midnight when she slipped into my room. She said that Jake had come home early and gone straight to bed, and that if he knew what was good for him he'd stay there.

It was funny, her ordering him around. We were going to kill him, yet she was going right ahead scolding and fussing, threatening what she'd do if he didn't behave himself.

"Damn him, anyway," she whispered angrily. "I was never so scared in my life, Carl."

"Yeah," I said. "It gave me quite a jar, too."

"Why in the world do you suppose he did it?"

"Oh, I don't know. Like the doctor said probably, so mixed up and screwed up he doesn't know what he's doing."

"Yeah, but...but gosh! Whew, I was scared!"

I didn't tell her about Kendall. I had nothing to gain by it, and a hell of a lot to lose. She might say something or do something that would tip him off. Or she might...well, I didn't like to think about that but I had to: The fact that she might not be on, or stay on, the level with me.

Kendall had saved my neck this morning. He couldn't have done it if Jake had been wise to him. And if I needed help from Kendall in the future and Jake *was* wise to him...

You see? Kendall was The Man's ace in the hole...*dammit, he just about had to be.* But he was mine, too, up to a point. As long as I kept my nose clean with The Man Kendall was on my side...*he didn't have to be; he could be leading me on, trying to get me to tip my hand.* I couldn't open up with him. I couldn't lay it on the line with her.

The only person I could trust was Charlie Bigger, Little Bigger. And that sawed-off son-of-a-bitch, I was beginning to have some doubts about him.

Talk about Jake being on a spot. Compared to me, Jake didn't have anything to worry about.

...It was a pretty chilly night, and she'd gotten into bed with me. We lay close together, whispering when we had anything to say, her head pillowed on my arm.

"I'd better start getting used to doing without you," I said. "We can't keep this up, baby. If there's something we have to talk over, sure; we'll risk it. Otherwise, we stay out of the clinches."

"But...but it'll be months, Carl! You mean we've got to wait all that time until—"

"Maybe not. I guess not," I said. "Like I said, there'll be times we have to get together. But we'll have to hold 'em down, Fay. The more we're together, the more chances that someone will find out about it."

"I know, honey. I know we have to be careful."

"Another thing"—I suddenly remembered something. "Those amytal capsules. Why in the name of God did you buy them, kid?"

"Well...he uses so damned many of them, and they cost so much if you go to a doctor and get a prescription—"

"Don't try to save dough that way again," I said. "The stuff is poison. You buy it without a prescription, and he accidentally takes an overdose—"

"Whew!" she shivered. "Why—why someone else might slip him a load and I—I'd—"

She left the sentence unfinished.

At last she snickered softly. I gave her a pat...and took a long deep breath.

"Something funny?"

"That Ruth! Every time I think about it I want to burst out laughing."

"Yeah," I said. "That's a riot, all right."

"Ugh. It makes me kind of sick to think about it. What in the world would anyone—what could he be like, Carl?"

"I wonder," I said.

14

I was up and dressed early the next morning, but I didn't go downstairs right away. I'd started to when I remembered about Ruth, about being alone with her—and I *would* have been alone with her at that hour. So I sat down on the edge of the bed and waited. Smoking and fidgeting. Feeling pretty queasy and nervous about getting started in school—Christ, imagine me in school!—but wanting to get it over with.

I waited, listening for Kendall's door to open. Then, I waited a few seconds more, so it wouldn't look like I *had* been waiting for him, and headed for my door.

He knocked on it, just as I turned the knob.

"Ah, good morning, Mr. Bigelow," he said. "All ready to begin your college career?"

"Yes, sir. I guess I am," I said.

"Such enthusiasm," he laughed sympathetically. "A little nervous, eh? A feeling of strangeness and unreality? Well, that's natural enough. Do you know, I have half a notion to—uh—"

"Yes, sir?"

"Would you regard it as—uh—presumptuous if I accompanied you? I am rather well acquainted with the faculty, and possibly as my—uh—er—protégé you might feel somewhat more—"

"I wish you would," I said. "I can't think of anything I'd like better."

"Really?" He seemed pleased as all get out. "I—I feel very flattered, Mr. Bigelow. I was going to suggest it last night, but I was afraid it might seem an intrusion."

"I wanted to ask you," I said. "But it seemed like a pretty nervy thing to do."

"Tsk, tsk," he beamed. "We must be less—uh—diffident with one another from now on. How about breakfast, eh? I seem to have an unusually hearty appetite this morning."

I didn't know. I'd been practically sure yesterday, but now he had me wondering again.

He could be both things. The nice, dignified, little old guy and the other, too. You can do that, split yourself up into two parts. It's easier than you'd think. Where it gets tough is when you try to get the parts back together again, but...He didn't need to be pretending. Most of the time I'd never pretended I'd really like a guy or want to help him along, but I'd go right ahead and—and do what I had to.

Well, anyway, I was damned glad he was going with me. It seemed funny, with all the other things I had to worry me, that I'd been uneasy about getting enrolled in a hick college. But I just couldn't help it. I guessed maybe it went back to the days when Luke and me and the rest of us had been crop tramps, and maybe you'd get two days in a school one week and three days a month in another. You never knew a thing about the lessons, and you smelled kind of bad and maybe you had a head full of lice, and you'd get put way off somewhere by yourself. You couldn't see worth a damn and your teeth had screwed up your hearing, and there was nothing you could do that someone didn't laugh at you or lay into you. And...

Skip it. Forget it. I was just trying to explain why I felt like I did.

Ruth served breakfast to us, and the way she kept trying to catch my eye I had a notion to take it out and hand it to her.

If she hadn't been kind of awed by Kendall, I think she might have suggested walking to the college with me. Shy as she was, much as she hated to show herself on that crutch.

She seemed to have it that bad.

I wondered whether there wasn't some safe way of getting Fay to give her the gate. And I guessed there was, probably, but I knew I wasn't going to do it. I'd tell her where to head in if I got the chance — if I had to.

But I wouldn't get her fired.

Kendall finally finished eating — I'd just been dragging my breakfast out, waiting for him — and we got started. I hadn't thought much about what courses I would take. I didn't know the score on those things, naturally, and I'd just supposed that you wouldn't have much say-so about your studies.

Kendall said it wouldn't be that way.

"That would be somewhat the case if you were a regular member of the freshman class or if you were majoring in a specific subject. But since you'll be classified as a special student—you're attending as a matter of self-improvement and for, I assume, the prestige value of college study—you have a great deal of latitude as to subjects. Now if you wouldn't— uh—if you would like my suggestions—"

"I certainly would," I said.

"Something, then, which would not point up any shortcomings in your past schooling. Something that is not predicated upon earlier studies in the same field...English literature. One can appreciate Pope without ever having read a line of Dryden. Political Science—more a matter of common sense than doctrinaire. History—merely another branch of literature...How does that sound to you, Mr. Bigelow?"

"Well—it sounds pretty—"

"Impressive? Impressive is the word." He chuckled, pleased with himself. "With such a course, no one could doubt your seriousness as a student."

Impressive wasn't the word I'd been thinking of. I'd been about to say it sounded pretty damned tough.

"Whatever you say," I said. "If you think I can get by in those things."

"You can and shall...with perhaps some slight assistance from me. You may depend upon it, Mr. Bigelow, I would not suggest subjects for you in which you could not—uh—get by."

I nodded. I didn't think I'd have much trouble getting by either.

With someone like Kendall to steer me—someone who knew the ropes—I couldn't miss.

I imagine I could have got the enrollment over in thirty minutes, and I did get my registration over and my fees paid in about that time. But Kendall wasn't through when that was done. He introduced me to the president and the chancellor and the dean of men—and they were all polite and respectful to him. Then, he took me around and introduced me to each of the instructors I'd have.

When noon came we still had one more guy to see, so we ate in the school cafeteria and looked him up after lunch. By the time we got through with him it was two o'clock, and Kendall said there wasn't much point in starting any classes that day.

"Let's see, now"—he glanced at his watch as we left the campus—"why don't you use the rest of the afternoon to pick up any books or supplies you need? Then, after dinner, around six-thirty, say…Would that be agreeable, Mr. Bigelow? I was thinking we might set your working shift at, loosely, six-thirty to eleven."

"Couldn't I come in earlier than that?" I said. "I won't need more than an hour or so to do my shopping, and after today I'll be out of my class at three. I'd like to come in earlier, Mr. Kendall. For a while, anyway."

I sounded plenty sincere—like maybe Dick Doordie, fighting through to fortune—and that's just how I felt. Until Ruthie cooled off, I had to have some place to hang out.

"Well—uh—of course, there wouldn't be any more money for you, but…"

"I don't care about that," I said. "I just like to be doing something, learning something."

He turned his head slowly and looked at me, and for a moment I thought he was going to ask who the hell I was kidding. And when he finally got around to speaking, he seemed so pleased he was all choked up.

"Mr. Bigelow, I—I can't tell you how glad I am that you came to Peardale. My only regret is that we could not have met—that the circumstances of our association could not have been—uh—"

He broke off, blowing his nose, and we walked a block before he said anything more.

"Well, we must take things as we find them, eh? We must look on the bright side. You are industrious, you have fortitude, the will-to-do, and now you are doing all that can be done to round out your education...A powerful triumvirate, my s— Mr. Bigelow, flawed and shadowed as it may be. When you consider someone like poor Ruth, whose sole assets virtually are ambition and a quick mind—and handicapped as she is they are doubtful assets indeed—your own situation seems one of great good fortune."

"I'm not complaining," I said. "You say Ruth's pretty smart?"

"Brilliant. Far from worldly-wise, of course, but an exceptionally keen intelligence. An honor student at the college. She's very well thought of there, incidentally. If you should encounter some difficulty with the curriculum, I'm sure she'd be glad to—"

"I wouldn't want to bother her," I said. "She gets embarrassed so easily. I don't want to pester you either, of course, but if I do have any trouble I'd rather talk it over with you. I feel more— well, more at home with you."

"Hem!" He swelled up like a poisoned pup. "Splendid— uh—that is to say, excellent! A pleasure, Mr. Bigelow."

We separated down near the middle of town. He headed for the bakery, and I picked up my school supplies, taking a fast gander at Jake's barber shop as I passed it. It was a two-chair joint, but a cloth was draped over the front chair. Jake was dozing in the rear one, his head drooped forward on his chest.

I finished my buying, and had some coffee in a drugstore. Going out the door, I ran head on into Sheriff Summers.

"Howdy there, son." He stood back from me a little. "Thought you'd be in school today."

"I've been there most of the day," I said. "Mr. Kendall went with me to see that I got off on the right foot, and we met so many of his friends I was all day in registering."

"Well, well. Kendall went with you, eh? Didn't think nothin' short of a three-ring circus could get him away from that bakery."

"I'm on my way to work there now," I said. "I've just been picking up some things I need at school."

"Swell. Good boy." He clapped me on the back. "Uh—kinda hopin' I might run into you. Bessie's been—I mean, how about eatin' with us this Sunday?"

"Well"—I hesitated—"I... If you're sure it wouldn't be any trouble for you, sheriff."

"Nothin' like it," he said heartily. "Tickled to death to have you. How'd it be if we meet you at church and go right from there?"

I said that would be fine.

"We'll be lookin' forward to it, then. I'm doggone glad you're gettin' lined up so well, son, after that—after all that mess at the beginning. Just keep up the good work, huh?"

"Thank you," I said. "I certainly intend to, sheriff."

I passed Jake's shop again on the way to the bakery. And there he was, standing right up against the glass, staring straight out at me.

I could feel him watching me all the way up the street.

I put my books in my locker at the bakery, and changed clothes. I went up the stairs, whistling, feeling about as happy as a guy like me could feel. I knew I had plenty to worry about, and it wasn't any time to be getting cocky and careless. But the way things had gone today—getting squared away at school and the sheriff warming up to me and...and everything—I just couldn't worry much.

Kendall spotted me the moment I hit the floor, and he was all business now.

"Come along, Mr. Bigelow," he said, herding me toward the stockroom. "I'll get you started off, and then I'll have to leave you."

We entered the stockroom, the main one, and he handed me the batch cards. There were fourteen of them—cardboard oblongs a little wider than a cigarette package and about three times the length. Each one listed the quantity and kind of ingredients wanted for a dough batch: bread, cake, piecrust, dough-nuts and so on.

"Read them all, all right, Mr. Bigelow? Everything clear to you? Let me see you set up the sponge on that whole-wheat bread mix."

I picked out the card, and shoved the others into my pocket. I looked at the list of ingredients and started for the substoreroom. Then, I remembered and picked up a pail instead.

"That's right," he smiled briskly. "The flour's just there for the record; they can draw that themselves. Pretty hard to over or under-draw on sacked flour. All you're concerned with is the sponge. Sugar, first, remember. Then —"

I remembered.

I scooped sugar from a barrel and weighed it on the scales. I dumped it into the pail, and weighed in salt and powdered milk. I wiped the scales clean, dribbled some of the plaster-of-Paris compound on them, and emptied it into a glassine bag. I tucked the bag into the pail, up against the side of it. Then I carried the pail into the cold-storage room.

I'd worked up a light sweat, but it was gone the second I stepped inside. He stood watching me, holding the door open.

There was another set of scales in there. I weighed lard onto them and dumped it into the pail. I punched a depression in the lard with my fist, measured a pint of malt syrup into the depression, and carried the pail outside. Kendall let the door slam shut, nodding approvingly.

"Very good, Mr. Bigelow. Just drop the batch card in at the side, there, and you have it done... Now about that door — you can't be too careful about that. Be very sure it's off the latch when you go in, or better still block it open slightly. One of those barrel scrapers should do the job."

"I'll be careful, all right," I said.

"Please do. You'll be here alone most of the time. You could be locked in there several hours before you were discovered, and it would be of very little use to discover you even after a much briefer lapse of time. So...Oh, yes. Speaking of doors."

He motioned to me, and I followed him into the substoreroom. He led me to the street door—the one he'd hinted I might use as a private entrance—pulling out a key ring.

"I've had a key made for you"—he took it off the ring. "We receive flour and other supplies through this door, so regardless— uh—So you'll doubtless find use for it. We'll just see how it works, now, and—"

It didn't fit too well, apparently. Kendall had to twist it back and forth and push up on the knob before the door finally opened.

"Well," he frowned. "I suppose we'll have to make it do for the time being. Perhaps with use—"

His mouth came shut, tightening with distaste. I looked across the street where he was looking—staring—and I saw Jake Winroy duck his head quickly and speed up that sagging, lopsided lope of his by a notch or two.

He passed out of viewing range.

Kendall slammed the door, jerked on the knob, testing it, and handed me the key.

"I don't know"—he shook his head—"I don't know that I've ever met anyone I so thoroughly detested. Well, we can't waste our valuable time on him, can we? Any questions? Anything that's not clear to you? If not, I'll get back to the floor."

I said I thought I had everything down pat, and he left.

I went back to the main stockroom.

I lined up all the sponge pails in a row, measured the dry ingredients into each of them, and carried them into the cold-storage room. I measured in the lard and malt, tucked in the batch cards, and set the pails just outside the entrance to the baking room.

I came back into the stockroom, studying the cards for the sweet doughs.

I was kind of breathless. I didn't need to, but I'd been rushing my head off. Not out here, but in there. In the cold-storage room.

I lighted a cigarette, telling myself I'd better take it easier. I wouldn't last long, rushing. Hard work—steady hard work—well, I'd given my lifetime quota on that a long time ago.

Aside from that, it would be easy to screw things up if I hurried too fast. I didn't know the job good yet. Working with all those different ingredients and measurements, a guy wouldn't have to be even pretty careless to get a little too much of one thing and not enough of another. And there wouldn't be any way of spotting the mistake until the stuff came out of the ovens—as hard as brick-bats maybe or as tough as shoe leather.

I glanced at the cold-storage room, and I shivered a little. So it was cold. What of it? I didn't need to stay in there, like I'd done on the sponges, wrapping up everything at one time. I could stay in, say, for five minutes, come out and go back in again for another five. Why stay in there, freezing my tail off, trying to do everything at once?"

I knew why, and I made myself admit it. The goddam place kind of gave me the creeps. I wanted to get through in there as fast as I could. It was so damned quiet. You'd hear a noise and sort of start, and then you'd realize that you'd gulped or one of your muscles had creaked and that was the noise you'd heard.

The door was so thick and heavy that you seemed locked in even when you knew you weren't. You kept looking at the scraper to see if it was still in place. And everything was kind of greasy and damp in there—everything seemed about the same shade—and you could look two or three times and still not be sure.

If you could have propped the door wide open—but you couldn't do that. Kendall had warned me about keeping the door open any more than was necessary. It would be a hell of a cold-storage room if you did that much.

I coughed, choked back another cough. The bug wasn't active again, I was sure of that, but I was glad I hadn't had to produce a health certificate.

I dropped the cigarette butt, stepped on it, and looked at the cards for the sweet doughs. They were more complicated than the others, the sponge mixes, and the extra-refined flour had to be weighed out with the other ingredients. They didn't just draw what they wanted as they did on the bread.

If I took my time on this stuff—and I'd damned well better—I probably wouldn't have it ready a hell of a lot sooner than I had to.

I took the scraper out of my pocket. I pulled the cold-storage room door open, and went inside. I laid the scraper handle against the jamb, letting the door settle against it. Then I turned my back on the damned thing and got busy.

There were eight batches in all. I decided to do two, and go out and get the dry stuff ready for them. Then, I'd come back and do two more, and so on until I was through. And if I didn't like it in here, I knew what to do about it. There was an easy way to save time. I could snap out of the creeps and stop checking on the door every ten seconds.

I got busy, I put two pans on the work table, leaned their batch cards against them, and began pouring and dumping and weighing. And the creeps stayed right with me, but I didn't give in to them. I never looked once at the door.

The work went pretty fast. It didn't seem to, but according to my watch it did. I finished the first two batches — the wet part of them — took them out and set up the dry stuff, and came back in again.

I did another two and another two. And started on the fourth pair. The last two I had to do.

I got them done, and somehow they seemed to take longer than the others. It seemed like I'd never get through with them. Finally, though, they were ready, and I tucked the batch cards into the slits at the end of the pans.

Then, I picked them up and turned around and pushed against the door.

I pushed — pretty easy at first. Easy because I couldn't bring myself to push hard. I just sort of leaned against it, because if I did more than that — if I pushed hard and it *didn't*...

I put a little more steam into it; just a little. And then a little more...and a little more.

And then suddenly I wasn't pushing, hard or any other way. I was throwing myself at it, giving it every thing I had. And I was still holding onto those mixes, why the hell I don't know, and they were slopping all over me and the floor. And I hit that door like I was going to drive straight through it. And I bounced and skidded and slipped. And I did a belly whopper to the floor.

The wind went out of me like a popped balloon. I gagged and retched but nothing came up. I lay on the floor, writhing, squeezing my head between my hands, trying to squeeze the pain away. And after a while I could breathe again, and I could get my eyes to focus.

I looked. The door was closed tight.

The scraper wasn't there, and it hadn't slipped inside. Someone had taken it away.

15

I laughed. I got ahold of the table and pulled myself up. I laughed and laughed, brushing at the crap on my clothes, feeling it cling and stick and stiffen against my fingers.

Because what was the sense to it anyway? How in the hell could you win? You were right on the beam — playing all the angles, doing things twice as well as you thought you could and getting some breaks thrown in. Everything was swell, and you were a bright boy and a tough boy.

And a punchy booze-stupe without enough guts to string a uke could come along and put the blocks to you.

He could do it because he *didn't* have anything. Nothing to lose. He didn't need to be smart, to cover his tracks. You had to cover them for him. He could make one dopey move after another, and all you could do was duck and keep your mouth shut. He didn't need guts. He could run from you, but you couldn't run from him. He could pick you off any way, any time, and if he got caught...? I had to choose between times and ways, and if I got caught...? Not responsible? Not a chance. If you beat the law there was still The Man.

I laughed and choked and coughed. It was such a hell of a good joke, me feeling sorry for Jake.

That was my first reaction — that it was the damnedest funniest thing in the world and it was a relief to get it all over. It hadn't made any sense from the beginning. I'd go right on looking for whatever I was looking for, and I wouldn't stand any better chance of finding it than I ever had.

So it was funny. It was a relief.

Then that cold really began to gnaw into me, and I stopped laughing and I wasn't relieved any more.

It was too simple, too clear-cut and easy. I'd been swimming in muck all my life, and I could never quite sink in it and I could never quite get to the other side. I had to go on, choking to death a little at a time. There wouldn't be anything for me as clean and easy as this.

I looked at my watch. I got up and started walking back and forth, stamping my feet, rubbing my hands and slapping them against my body.

Four-thirty. It seemed like it ought to be hours later than that, I'd done so much that day and got started so early, but it was only four-thirty... Kendall would knock off at a quarter of six to go to the house for dinner, and he'd come in after me. And then I'd get out of here.

No one would come in before then. There wasn't any reason for them to, and — and they just wouldn't. And Kendall wouldn't dress out without me, and go on to the house by himself.

Either way, see, would make it easy for me, and that was

against the rules. I wouldn't be found soon enough to really help, or late enough to . . . to do any good.

Four-thirty to five-forty-five. An hour and fifteen minutes. That would be the score. No more, no less. Not enough to kill me; too much, a hell of a lot too much, to leave me unharmed. Just the right amount to knock me on my ass.

I should have given up, just relaxed and stopped trying to do anything about it. Because whatever I did or didn't do, I wasn't going to change a thing. I'd still be just *so* sick, *almost* completely screwed up, not *quite* stripped of everything I had. Right at the time when I needed everything I had and I couldn't be screwed up at all.

No, I couldn't change a thing. But I had to try.

Relaxing, giving up, those were against the rules, too.

I walked back and forth, stamping and slapping and pounding, hugging my arms across my chest, sticking my hands between my crotch and clasping my legs on them. And I kept getting colder and stiffer, and my lungs began to feel like I was breathing fire.

I climbed up on the table, trying to warm my hands against the light in the ceiling. But there was a wire guard around it, and it was just a little globe, and it didn't do any good.

I climbed back down and started walking again. Trying to think . . . A fire? Huh-uh. Nothing to burn, and it wouldn't do anyway. It wouldn't even be smart to smoke. The air wasn't too good now.

I looked along the rows of shelves, looking—for anything. I studied the labels on the thick jugs: Extract of Vanilla, Extract of Lemon... *Alcohol 40 per cent*... But I knew better than that, too. You'd feel warmer for a few seconds, and then you'd be colder than ever.

I began to get sore. I thought, for Christ's sake, what kind of a dope are you, anyway? You're supposed to be smart, remember? You don't just take things. You don't like something, you do something about it. Locked up, not locked up. It's still the same, isn't it, except for the air. Suppose...

Suppose you were riding that manifest out of Denton, the fast meat train that balls the jack all the way into El Reno. It's November and all the goddamned reefer boles are locked, so you're riding the top, in the goddamn cold wind. And you can't die, and you'd better not get down. Because you remember that kid in the jungle at St. Joe, the color of the weeds he was lying in; taking on the boes for a dime or a nickel or a cart of coffee or... So?

I remembered. I didn't invent the trick but it's a good one:

You crawl down inside your cotton sack, the sack you pick cotton into. It's nine feet long and made out of canvas, and you kind of flap the end over itself so that just a tiny bit of air comes in. And you breathe practically the same air in and out, but you warm up fast. After a while your lungs start itching and smarting and your head begins to hurt. But you stay there, keeping your mind on warm things, warm and soft, and safe...

I didn't have a cotton sack now, of course, or anything in the way of a big piece of cloth. But if I could get inside of something, pull something over me, and put my breath to work...well, it would help. I took a long careful look around the room.

Egg can? Too small. Lard barrel? Too big; it would take too long to dig the lard out. Mincemeat...?

The keg was only about a fourth full. I squatted down, trying to measure myself against it, and it was pretty small—not really what I ought to have. But it was the only thing I did have.

I turned it upside down, then got my arms around it and banged it up and down, dumping the sweet-smelling, semi-frozen slush on the floor. I scraped the inside with a scoop, and I knew I could scrape all night and not get it completely clean. So I gave up and got it over me.

I sat down on the floor with my arms at my sides, and stuck my head and shoulders into it. Then, I sat up and let it slide down over me. It only came down to my hips, and little gobs of that goo kept letting go and trickling down onto me. But that had to be it—it and me was all I had. So I breathed hard and tried to concentrate on...on warmness and softness, comfort and safety.

I got to thinking about the farm that guy had up in Vermont, where he grew all those things. And I remembered how he'd said that he didn't have any demand any more except for just the one thing. I closed my eyes, and I could almost see them, the long rows of them. And I grinned and laughed to myself, beginning to feel kind of good and pretty warm. And then I thought, I began to see:

...*the goats were going up and down the rows, walking sideways on their hind feet. And every time they came to one they'd raise their tails and cut loose with the fertilizer. And each time*

they came to the end of a row they'd stand on their heads and howl.
They had to do it. They knew it wasn't going to get them anything
because there was nothing there to get, but they kept right on.
Moving sideways and backwards—because that was the way the
rows were laid out. And at the end they stood on their heads,
howling...

I stopped thinking about it.

There was no warmth in it.

I brought my mind back to Kendall, him and Fay. Wondered
what I'd better tell them. And I knew I'd better not tell the
truth.

She might blow up—jump Jake about it or give it away to
someone else. She might scare off. If she got sore or shaky, if she
thought Jake could take the ball away from me...

And Kendall. If he was on the level, he'd have Jake in jail so
fast it would make his head swim. He'd gotten a bang out of the
other, the frame-up, because nothing had come of it and he'd
outsmarted Jake. But if he thought Jake had tried to kill me,
and *if* he was on the level, he couldn't let it slide. He'd have to
crack down to protect the bakery.

If he was with The Man—that would be worse yet. The Man
already thought I might have a few rocks in my head. He'd been
sore about me dragging in Fay and... *why, in hell had I done*
that, anyhow? I could have got along without her... He probably
had a hunch that I might have seen through that Fruit Jar fram-
mis and didn't trust him as much as I had to trust him. And if
he thought I couldn't do any better than this, get it thrown into
me by the guy I was supposed to throw it into...

No, it had to be an accident. That would be bad enough.

...I twisted my wrist and looked down. Five-twenty. About twenty-five minutes to go. An hour and fifteen minutes plus the time before I'd got locked in. It wouldn't be enough for a guy in good health. He'd have the sniffles and a sore throat, and that would be about the size of it. With me, though, it would be exactly enough. I couldn't have timed it better if I'd been trying to knock myself out.

Twenty-four minutes...

Ruth. As long as I'd known I was going to use Fay, why had I made a play for Ruth?

And Fay; getting back to Fay. It wouldn't have been any wonder—I wouldn't have blamed The Man much—if he'd given Fruit Jar that knife instead of me.

Sure, Fay could be a big help. Sure, she could make things a lot easier for me. So what? She could do something else, too. If she was smart enough to see it. Because how can you really trust a dame who'll help kill her own husband?

The Man had told me what she could do; he'd pointed out the spot where I could go down and never come up. He'd just mentioned it once, then he'd let it lay and gone on. Fay was already in or as good as in, and there was nothing to do but like it. But he wouldn't have been The Man if he *had* liked it. Brother, he must have thought I was a goof!

Me—Little Bigger—putting the one rope in the world around my neck that would hang me!

I didn't have a record, none that they could pin on me. I could line up before every cop in the country and there wasn't a one that could say, yes, that's our Bigger boy. No one could say it and prove it.

No one could, now.

But if I could be caught in the act of trying to kill Jake Winroy — if they had that much to go on, and could work back from it...

All those rewards, all for Fay. Forty-seven thousand dollars for Fay...and no half-blind runt with a mouth like a dog's behind to get in her hair.

...I got out just about on schedule. Kendall found me around ten minutes of six, and he and one of the bakers got me home. By six-thirty I was in bed with two hot-water bottles, feeling sort of drowsy and dopey from something the doctor had given me.

It was the same doctor — Dodson — that Fay had called for Jake. But he wasn't at all crusty and tough with me like he'd been with him and her. My own moth...you couldn't have wanted a guy to be nicer.

He pulled the blankets back up over my chest, and tucked them under my chin.

"So you're feeling fine, huh? No pain at all...Never mind. I don't want you talking with that throat."

I grinned at him, and my eyelids began to droop shut. He turned and gave Fay a nod.

"I want this boy to rest. He is to have complete quiet, understand? No nonsense. No disturbance such as occurred here yesterday."

"I" — Fay bit her lip, blushing — "I understand, doctor."

"Good. See that your husband does. Now, if you'll get that bedpan I spoke to you about a quarter of an hour ago —"

She went out.

The doctor and Kendall moved over near the door.

And I wasn't quite asleep yet, I was just drifting off. And I got a little of what they said.

"...all right?"

"This time. Stays in bed, and... Ought to be up by..."

"...relieved to... strong personal interest..."

"Yep. This time... wouldn't bet a nickel on..."

"...pessimist, Dod. Why a next..."

"...teeth out... lens. No, better do it my..."

"...don't mean he...?"

"...everything. Straight across the board... nothing really right... no good to begin..."

That was the last I heard.

16

I was in bed until Friday. Or, I should say, I didn't leave the house until then, because I didn't stay in bed all the time. When I had to vomit or use the toilet I went to the bathroom, and I made sure that everything was flushed down good.

I told everyone that I felt all right—that I was just sort of weak and tired. And aside from all that blood and phlegm, which began tapering off about Thursday, there *didn't* seem to be a hell of a lot wrong with me. I didn't have much pain. Like I said, I was just weak and tired. And I had a funny feeling that a lot of me had been taken away.

What there was of me was all right, but there wasn't much of me any more.

Fay spent a lot of time in my room. And that was okay, of course, since she was supposed to take care of me. We had plenty of time to talk.

She said that Jake had been in the house and in bed every night by eleven o'clock. As she put it, he was behaving like a perfect lamb.

"How about that, anyway?" I asked her, making it sound

casual. "I mean, how come he lets you boss him around? What's he afraid of?"

She shrugged. "Gosh, I don't know, honey. Afraid I'll leave him, I guess."

"It's not doing him a hell of a lot of good for you to stay."

"No?" She laughed huskily, slanting her eyes at me. "Now how would you guess a thing like that?"

I let the talk drift off onto other things — what a funny little guy Kendall was and who in the hell could have seduced Ruthie — and after a while I let it drift back to Jake again.

"This board money doesn't amount to anything," I said, "and I don't see how he can make any dough in that shop of his. How do you keep going?"

"You call this going?"

"It takes dough. Quite a bit with Jake hitting the whiz so hard."

"We-el, he does have *some* business, Carl. Me" — she guffawed and put her hand over her mouth — "I'd be afraid I'd get scalped. But everyone knows him and knew his folks, and he has some trade. On Fridays and Saturdays, you know, when all the shops are busy. And he's usually hanging around there, at night, staying open, when the other shops are closed."

One day — Wednesday, I think it was, when she brought my lunch up — I asked her if Jake had ever mentioned going back to jail.

She shook her head firmly. "For ten years? He couldn't take it when he was being paid off heavy — when he knew he'd be taken care of when he got out. They wouldn't play with him any more, would they, Carl? If he was willing? He'd just do his time and they'd get him when it was over?"

I nodded. "If they couldn't arrange to get him inside...Why in hell did he do it anyway, Fay? I know the cops probably shot him a big line about how they'd protect him and no one would dare touch him because it just wouldn't be good business, but—"

"And how! I hated to lose out on that payoff money, but I didn't think—no one seemed to think that—"

"Jake must have known how it would be. Hell, look at the way he started slipping. Hitting the jug and letting himself go. Look at the way he blew up when he spotted me."

"Yeah. Well—" She shook her head again. "Why do we do anything? He was going nuts in jail. He felt like he'd been the fall guy for the rest of the crowd, and the money he was getting wasn't doing *him* any good. So—"

That was about the size of the matter. I knew it. I'd been briefed on every phase of the deal, just what had happened and why and how it had happened.

But I wanted her to tell me, anyway.

"Why doesn't he turn himself into custody? Stay in the jug until after the trial is over?"

"Why?" She frowned at me, puzzled.

"That's what I said. If he's so sure I'm—someone's going to bump him off to keep him from talking, why—?"

"But, honey. What good would that do? They'd get him afterwards."

"Yeah, sure," I said. "That's the way it would be, all right." Her frown deepened a little.

"Honey… You're not — not getting nervous, are you?"

"About him?" I forced a laugh. "Not a chance. He's in the bag and I'm all set to sew it up."

"How? Tell me, Carl."

I hadn't meant to tell her so soon. The safest way would have been to keep it to myself right up to the last minute. But — well, I'd got her a little worried with all that questioning. And it looked to me like I'd better show her I was right on the ball before she got more worried.

"Here's the deal," I said. "We'll pick a weekend night when Ruth's gone home to her folks, and —"

She, Fay, would set Jake up. She'd meet him downtown earlier and see that he didn't get too much to drink. Then she'd go on home, after she had him good and teased up, to get ready for what she'd promised to give him.

"Make him believe it," I said. "Make him want it so bad he can taste it. Know what I mean?"

"I know. Go on, Carl."

"Okay. You go on home. He gives you a few minutes, and then he follows you. I'll be watching at the door of the bakery, and I follow him. I catch up with him at the steps, pop his neck and drop him off on his head. I beat it back to the bakery, and you discover him. You heard him stumble, see, like he's always stumbling on those steps. That's it."

"How will you — his neck —?"

"It's easy. You don't have to worry about that."

"Well, gosh. It — it sounds so … so simple!"

"You want it hard?"

"Well, no—" Her frown went away and she laughed. "When do we do it, Carl?"

"I'll let you know. Not for weeks yet."

"Gee," she said, wonderingly. "Imagine me thinking you might be getting a little sca—worried!"

"Are you kidding?" I said.

"Gee," she said, again. "You tough little bastard, you!"

...Kendall was in to see me at least twice a day. He fussed around over me like I was a two-year-old kid, feeling my forehead and asking me if I didn't want this or that or the other, then kind of scolding me about smoking too much and not taking better care of myself.

"You really must, Mr. Bigelow. So much depends on it," he'd say.

And I'd say, "Yes, sir, Mr. Kendall. I understand."

It seemed that quite a few guys had got themselves locked into the cold-storage room at one time or another, and he took it for granted that I'd done the same. He also took it for granted that I'd opened that side door of the bakery for some reason, and left it unlocked.

And, of course, I didn't correct him. I didn't point out that he'd done it himself when he was trying out the new key.

Kendall usually managed to be around when the doctor came to see me, but he and the doc didn't do much talking after the first couple visits. Kendall didn't want to be told that I was in bad shape, and Dodson apparently wasn't a guy to pull his punches. So, after the first couple visits, when Kendall argued with him and kept calling him a pessimist, the doctor got sort of grim and clammed up. About all he'd say was I'd be all right this time—*but*. "But," he'd say, and let it go at that.

And Kendall would be pretty red-faced and huffy, and almost glare at him until he got out of my room.

"A pessimist," he'd say, huffily. "Always looking on the dark side of everything…You *are* feeling better, aren't you, Mr. Bigelow?"

"Sure. Sure, I feel fine, Mr. Kendall," I'd say.

Thursday evening, he asked me about a dozen times if I was feeling better and if I was sure I should get up the next day… after that he got pretty quiet for a time. And when he spoke again it was about that little cabin he had up in Canada.

"It might be just the thing for you, Mr. Bigelow. In case, that is, that your health should worsen and you should not—uh—be able to carry out your plans here."

"I'm all right," I said. "I'll be able to carry them out, Mr. Kendall."

"I'm sure of it. It would indeed be tragic if you could not. But, in case…It would be ideal for you, Mr. Bigelow. You could take my car, and living would be very cheap and—I assume you have some money but I would be very happy to help—"

"I have most of what I got from my filling station," I said. "But it's awfully nice of you to offer—"

"Not at all. You're more than welcome to any help I can give you…What do you think about it, Mr. Bigelow, as a more or less pleasant solution to an unpleasant eventuality? You'd have complete quiet, the most favorable conditions for rest and study. The nearest town is forty miles away, accessible enough by car but far enough distant to insure your privacy. How does it sound to you, anyway?"

It sounded swell. I'd never heard of a better place to knock a guy off—as I was going to be knocked off if I fell down on the job here.

"That sounds nice," I said. "But I don't imagine I'll be going. I'm staying right here and going to school and—and do everything else I planned."

"Of course. Certainly," he nodded, and stood up to go. "It's just something to think about."

I thought about it.

It was almost one o'clock in the morning before I could get to sleep.

The next day, the day after that night, rather, was Friday. And I was still awfully weak and wrung out, but I knew I'd better not lie around any longer. Fay would start to worrying again. Kendall would start to wondering whether I could carry on or not. And if he had any doubts, it wouldn't be long until The Man had them.

I got up early, so that I could take my time about dressing, and ate breakfast with Kendall. I left the house when he did, and headed for the college.

That first morning—Monday morning—I hadn't paid any attention to the other students. I'd seen them, of course; some of them were passing us or we were passing them all the way to the school. But they hadn't made any impression on me. I mean, I hadn't been bothered by them. Kendall had been so free and easy that I'd felt the same way.

This morning, it was different. I felt like a jerk.

There was a regular parade of students going toward the college, and I was right in the middle of it. But somehow I wasn't part of it. I was always by myself, with the others in back or ahead of me, nudging each other when they thought I wasn't looking; laughing and whispering and talking. About my clothes, about the way I looked, about—everything. Because nothing about me was right...

I went to my first class, and the instructor acted like he'd never seen me before. He wanted to know if I was sure I was in the right class and why I was starting to school so late in the term. And he was one of those goofs who keep asking you questions without listening to your answers; and I had to explain, over and over, while the others sat grinning and watching me.

Finally, it sank in on him. He remembered about Kendall introducing me, and he halfway apologized for his forgetfulness. But things still weren't squared away. I'd been absent for three days, so I had to go to the dean of men for an okay before I could be admitted to classes.

I got it—a cut slip, I think they called it—and got back just about thirty seconds before the class was over. I was just sitting down in my seat when the bell rang.

Everyone got a big bang out of it. You'd have thought it was the funniest thing that ever happened.

In one class, I guess I must have moved a dozen times before I found a seat that didn't belong to someone else. I'd just get sat down when some dope would trail up and say it was where he sat. And, yeah, I think they were making a game out of it, trying to make me look dopier than I felt, but all I could do was keep moving until the instructor woke up and assigned me to a desk.

The third class, the one just before lunch, was the worst one. It was English literature, and everyone was taking turns at reading a few paragraphs aloud. So it came my turn, and the way I was looking down and talking at the same time, my teeth slipped a little bit. And everything I said sounded sort of like baby talk. The snickers and giggles got louder and louder, and finally the instructor told me to sit down.

"Very amusing, Bigelow," he said, giving me a glare that would have frosted an orchard. "Is Mr. Kendall acquainted with your talent for mimicry?"

I shrugged and smirked—what the hell could I do or say? And he frowned and nodded for another student to start reading. A little bit later—although it didn't seem like a little bit— the noon bell rang.

I stopped by his desk on the way out, and explained about the teeth. He was pretty nice about it, said he was sorry he'd misunderstood the situation and so on. So that was taken care of: he wouldn't knock me to Kendall. But...

I walked down the corridor to the building entrance, and everyone seemed to be laughing and talking about me. And part of it was imagination, of course, but not all of it. It was a small college, and I guess the students were pretty hard up for kicks, and news traveled fast.

I headed toward the house, wondering why in hell I bothered when I know I wouldn't be able to eat anything. I tried to keep to the side streets, dodging people whenever I could and cursing myself for doing it.

She ducked out of an alley just as I was ducking across it. Looking back, now, I'd say that she'd been waiting for me to pass.

I said. "Oh, hello, Ruth," and started to go on.

She said, "C-carl. Wait a minute."

"Yeah?" I said. I paused, waiting.

"I k-now you're mad at me about something, but—"

"Mad?" I said. "I don't even know you're alive."

"Y-yes," she said, "I know that, too. I didn't want to talk to you about that. All I wanted to say was about…about school. D-don't mind the way they act. Just go ahead, and after a while you get used to it."

She smiled, tried to. She nodded her head, and pivoted on her crutch.

And I knew that I should let her go like that, a clean hard break. But I couldn't do it. I stepped in front of her.

"I know you're alive, Ruthie," I said. "I know it plenty."

"N-no…I mean, it's all right, Carl. I—I guess, I just—"

"I've been trying to give you a break. I'm no good for you. I'm no good, period. But—"

"You are, too!" Her eyes flashed. "You're nice!"

"And there's Mrs. Winroy," I said. "I think she might be a little suspicious. If she thought there was anything going on between us, she'd probably fire you fast."

"Oh," she said, and her voice quavered a little. "I d-didn't… has she said anything? I couldn't lose my job, Carl! If I—"

176

"You'll have to watch it, then," I said. "That's why I've acted the way I have, Ruthie. It's the only reason. I like you a lot."

She stood blushing and trembling, the splayed hand gripping the brace of the crutch.

"That's the way it is, Ruth. Keep it in mind. I think you're pretty swell. If I don't show it, it's because I can't."

She nodded, looking like she was a dog and I owned her.

"Now, you can do me a little favor," I said. "If you want to. I'm feeling a little rocky, but I don't want to go back to the house and have everyone worrying over me, so —"

"Shouldn't you, Carl? I mean, don't you think you should stay in bed for another day?"

"I'm all right," I said, "but I don't think I feel up to school this afternoon. If you'll tell Kendall, or anyone else that asks, that I'm eating lunch at the cafeteria — don't let on, you know, that everything isn't okay —"

"It will be, Carl. You'll get used to it."

"Sure, I will," I said. "But I've had enough for today. I think I'll just loaf around town for a couple of hours, get myself pulled together before it's time to go to work."

She hesitated, frowning sort of troubled. "You're not...not awfully discouraged, Carl? You don't intend to drop out of school, and —?"

"Not a chance," I said. "Peardale's stuck with me, and I'm sticking with it. I just don't feel up to it this afternoon."

She went on, then, on down the alley, and I went on up the street to a nice quiet bar I'd spotted the day I was with Kendall.

I settled down in a rear booth, and I didn't move out of it until three o'clock.

I wouldn't have cared much if the sheriff or someone had spotted me there; they'd have had a hard time making anything out of the fact that I was taking things easy my first day out of bed. But no one came into the place that I knew. Hardly anyone came in at all, for that matter. So I just sat there, feeling more relaxed and rested the longer I sat, thinking and smoking and drinking.

I felt pretty good by the time I left.

What there was of me felt pretty good.

I got through my shift at the bakery. I put in a full eight hours there the next day, Saturday, and I got through them all right, too. So I got by all right. Just barely.

Because, like I said, there just wasn't a whole lot left of me.

I wondered what would happen if something tough came up, something really hard to take. Something that I couldn't handle in my own way, a little at a time, like I did the job.

And then it was Sunday, and I began to find out.

17

Sheriff Summers belched, and leaned back in his chair. "Fine dinner, Bessie," he said. "Can't remember when —*ughahh*—I et so much."

"At breakfast," said Mrs. Summers, wrinkling her forehead at him. "More coffee, Carl? I think, from the sound of things, that His Highness will have to settle for some baking soda and water."

"Aw, now, Bessie. Why—?"

"No, sir. Not another drop. And kindly stop picking at the meringue on that pie!"

The sheriff grinned sheepishly, and winked at me. "Ain't she a terror though, son? 'Bout the bossiest one woman you ever seen, I'll bet."

"I don't think I'd say that," I laughed.

"Certainly you wouldn't. Only His Highness is capable of it."

"He's just being polite." The sheriff winked at me again.

"But you're not, are you? Quiet. Carl and I do not care to talk to you, do we, Carl?"

"No, ma'am," I said, smiling.

And he and she laughed and smiled at me.

It was a nice day, any way you looked at it. Cool but sunny, just enough breeze to ripple the green-brown leaves of the trees. And it had got off to a good start. Kendall had let me set up most of my Sunday batches the day before and leave them in cold storage, and he'd insisted that I take all of today off. He'd really insisted, not in the way people do when they expect you to talk 'em out of it.

I was beginning to feel almost as much at home with the sheriff and his wife as I had with that old couple out in Arizona.

Sheriff Summers said he guessed he'd take a little nap, and Mrs. Summers told him by all means to go ahead. He went up to the front of the house where his bedroom was. She and I sat at the table a while longer, drinking coffee and talking. Then she took me outside to show me the yard.

Their house was one of those rambling old cottages which never seem to go out of date no matter how old they are. The yard was almost a half block wide and a block deep, and she'd tried to doll it up with flower beds and a rock garden in the rear.

I told her how I'd fixed up my little place in Arizona, and she said she could just see it and it sounded wonderful. We went from that to talking about the yard here, and hell, it had all kinds of possibilities. So I gave her a few suggestions, and she was tickled pink.

"That's marvelous, Carl! Will you come over and help me some time — some weekend, perhaps — if I pay you?

"No, ma'am," I said. "Not if you pay me."

"Oh. But really—"

"I'd enjoy doing it. I like to see things looking nice. I started to do a little work on the Winroy place—there's quite a few things, you know, that need—"

"I do know. Yes, indeed!"

"But I haven't felt like it was appreciated—more like I might be butting in. So I fixed the gate and let the other things slide."

"Those people. I'll bet they never even said thank you, did they?"

I shook my head. "For that matter, I guess I wanted to do the work more on my own account than theirs. The gate was the worst off, but those front steps have me worried too. Someone could get killed on those steps."

It was true. They were in lousy shape, and someone *could* get killed on them without any help. But I felt ashamed of myself for mentioning it. It was just that I always had to keep pointing so hard at one thing that everything coming out of me— everything I said or did—pointed at the one thing, also.

"Well," I said. "Speaking of work, I think it's time I was getting busy on those dinner dishes."

We'd been sitting on the back steps while we talked. I stood up and held out my hand to her.

She took it, and drew me back down on the steps.

"Carl—"

"Yes, ma'am," I said.

"I—I wish I could tell you how much I—" She laughed sort of crankily, as though she was scolding herself. "Oh just listen to me! I guess I've gotten like Bill, completely out of the habit of handing out bouquets. But…you know what I mean, Carl."

"I hope I do," I said. "I mean, I enjoy being with you and the sheriff so much I hope you—"

"We do, Carl. We've never had any children, no one but ourselves to think about. Perhaps that's been the…well, no matter. What can't be cured must be endured. But I've thought—I seem to have had you on my mind ever since last Sunday, and I've thought that if things had been different, if we'd had a son, he'd have been just about your age now. H-he—he'd be like… if he was like I've always pictured him…he'd be like you. Someone who was polite and helpful and didn't think I was the world's biggest bore, and—"

I couldn't say anything. I didn't trust my voice…Me, *her* son! *Me!*…And why couldn't it have been that way, instead of the way it was?

She was talking again. She was saying that she'd been "so angry at the way Bill acted last Sunday."

"It was all right," I said. "He has to be pretty careful in the job he's got."

"Careful, fiddlesticks!" she snapped. "It was not all right. I was never so angry in my life. I gave that man fits, Carl! I told him, 'Bill Summers, if you're going to be swayed by those Fields—someone who is obviously malicious and petty— instead of believing the evidence of your own eyes and ears, I'm—'"

"The Fields!" I turned and looked at her. "What Fields? The only Fields I know are dead."

"I'm talking about their son, him and his family. The relatives she lived with when she went back to Iowa. Bill wired them, you know, at the time he wired—"

"No," I said, "I didn't know. And maybe you'd better not tell me about it, Mrs. Summers. As long as the sheriff didn't, I don't think you should."

She hesitated. Then she said, softly, "You mean that, don't you, Carl?"

"I mean it," I said.

"I'm glad. I knew you'd feel that way. But he knows that I planned to tell you, and he doesn't object at all. The whole thing was so completely ridiculous in the first place! Even if he couldn't see the kind of young man you were at a glance, he had those wonderful wires about you from that judge and the chief of police and—"

"I don't understand," I said. "I don't know why this son would say anything against me. I couldn't have thought any more of a mother and father than I did of them. Why, Mrs. Fields wrote me right up to the time she died, and—"

"I imagine that was a large part of the trouble. Jealousy. And you know how kinfolk can be when it comes to elderly people. No matter what you do, how much you do, they're always convinced that you've abused the old folks. Imposed on them or swindled them or worse."

"But I—I just don't see how—"

"Honestly, Carl! Without ever having met you, I knew it was preposterous. They sent a five-hundred-word telegram back here, and it was simply filled with the worst possible...And, of course, Bill didn't just swallow it whole, but he didn't feel that he could disregard it completely. So — Oh, I suppose I shouldn't even have mentioned it. But it was so unfair, Carl, it made me so angry that—"

"Maybe you'd better tell me about it," I said. "If you don't mind."

She told me about it. I listened, sore at first, and then just sick. And I got sicker and sicker.

They—this Fields character—had said that I'd stolen his mother and father blind all the time I was working for them, and then I'd gypped her out of the station, paid her about half what the place was worth. He said I'd just moved in on his folks and taken over, and they'd been too scared of me to complain. He said—he hinted—that I'd actually killed Mr. Fields; that I'd made him do all the hard heavy work until he keeled over from heart failure. He said I'd planned to do the same thing to the old lady, but she'd taken what I offered her so I'd let her go "completely broken in health." He said...

Everything. Every lousy thing that a smalltime stinker could think of to say.

It was a lie, of course, every word of it. I'd worked for those people for peanuts, and I'd have stolen from myself quicker than I would have from them. I'd paid Mrs. Fields more than anyone else had offered when she put the place up for sale. I'd even done a big part of the housework for Mrs. Fields. I'd made Mr. Fields stay in bed, and I'd waited on him and done the other work besides. He'd hardly been out of bed for a year at the time he died, and she'd hardly stirred a hand, and...

And this character said things like that about me.

It made me sick. These people—those two people I'd cared more about than anything in the world, and…And this was the way it turned out.

Mrs. Summers touched my arm. "Don't feel badly, Carl. I know you were just as good and kind to those people as you could be and what *he* says doesn't change the facts."

"I know," I said. "I—" I told her how much I'd thought of the Fields and how I'd tried to show it, and she sat nodding sympathetically, murmuring an occasional, "Of course," and, "Why, certainly you did," and so on.

And pretty soon it seemed like I wasn't talking to her, by myself. I was arguing with myself. Because I knew what I'd done, but I wasn't sure why I had done it. I'd thought I was, but now I didn't know.

He was lying, of course; the way he'd put things had been a lie. But a lie and a truth aren't too far apart; you have to start with one to arrive at the other, and the two have a way of overlapping.

You could say I had moved in on the Fields. They hadn't really needed any help, and if they'd been younger and less good-hearted they probably wouldn't have given me a job. You could say that I had made them work hard. Two people could get by fine on the little business their station was doing, but three couldn't. And I'd saved them all the work I could, but still they'd had to work harder than they had before I came. You could say that I had stolen from them—just being there was stealing. You could say I had cheated Mrs. Fields on the price.

Because all I had I'd got from them, and the place was worth a lot more to me than it would have been to an outsider. You could say...

You could say that I'd planned it the way it had turned out; maybe without knowing that I was planning it.

I couldn't be sure that I hadn't. All I could be sure of was that I'd been fighting for my life, and I'd found the perfect spot— the one place—to take cover. I'd had to have what they had. In a way, it had been me or them.

Those six years I'd spent with them...Maybe they were like all the other years. Just crap. Nothing to feel kind of proud of or good about.

"Carl...Please, Carl!"

"I'm all right," I said.

"You're sick. I can see it. Now, you're coming right into the house with me and I'm going to fix you a cup of coffee, and you're going to lie down on the lounge until—"

"I think I'd better go home," I said.

I stood up and she stood up with me. And she looked almost as sick as I probably did. "Oh, I wish I hadn't told you, Carl! I might have known how upset you'd be."

"No, it's—I just think I'd better be going," I said.

"Let me call Bill. He can drive you."

"No, I'd rather you didn't," I said. "I—I want to walk around a little first."

She argued about it, looking and sounding like she might burst out crying any second. But finally she walked to the gate with me, and I got away.

I walked toward the house, the Winroys', my eyes stinging behind the contact lenses; and it didn't seem sunny or pleasant any more.

I could hear Ruthie out in the kitchen. No one else seemed to be around. I went out there, reached the whiskey out of the cupboard and took a long drink out of the bottle. I put it back in the cupboard, and turned around.

Ruthie was staring at me. She'd taken her hands out of the dishwater and was starting to reach for a towel. But somehow she never made it. She stared at me, and her face twisted as though a knife had been twisted in her; and she took a swing and a step on the crutch. Then her arms were around me and she was pressing me to her.

"C-carl...oh, darling. What's the—"

"Nothing," I said. "Just a little sick at my stomach."

I grinned and pulled away from her. I gave her a little spank on the thigh, and I started to say, I *did* say, "Where's—?" But I didn't get a chance to finish the sentence. I heard Fay coming up the front steps, that firm I'm-really-something walk of hers. And by the time she got the front door open, I was in the hallway.

I winked and jerked my head over my shoulder. "Just borrowed a drink of your whiskey, Mrs. Winroy. Had a sudden attack of stomach sickness."

"It's perfectly all right, Carl." She gave me back the wink. "Sick at your stomach, huh? Well, that's what you get for eating with cops."

"That's it," I laughed. "Thanks for the whiskey."

"Not at all," she said.

I started up the stairs. About halfway up, I suddenly turned around.

I wasn't quite sick enough to catch her at it; she was already entering the dining room. But I knew she'd been looking at me, and when I got to my room I found out why.

The back of my coat. The two white soapsuds prints of Ruthie's hands.

18

Fay was an actress. The Man had been right about that. I didn't know how much she'd been acting up until now, but she could have been doing it all the time. She was good, what I mean. A whole week had passed since she'd seen those hand-prints, and if I hadn't known that she *had* seen them, I'd never have guessed that there was anything wrong.

She'd come up to my room that night, that Sunday, and we'd kicked the gong around for almost an hour; and she'd never let on. We'd been together again on Wednesday—and I mean, *together*—and there still wasn't any indication that she knew. She'd never done or said anything to show that she was hell-hot sore.

She was waiting. She was going to let it all slide, convince me that she hadn't seen anything, before she made her move.

She waited a whole week, until the next Sunday night and...

That week.

I'd thought that school couldn't be any worse than it'd been that Friday, but it was. Maybe it just seemed worse because there was so much more of it and so much less of me.

That wire Mrs. Summers had told me about. This trouble with Fay. Ruthie. Kendall. Jake...

Jake was at the house for almost every meal. A couple of mornings he even ate breakfast with Kendall and me. He was still hitting the jug pretty hard, but he didn't seem to sag so much.

He seemed to be getting bigger, and I was getting littler. Every day there was a little bit less of me.

I said he was hitting the bottle pretty hard. But he wasn't even in it with me. I had to nail down my breakfast every morning with a few drinks before I could go to school. And I had to have more in the afternoon before I could get to work, and at night...

Thursday night I took a bottle up to my room with me, and I got half cockeyed. I got a notion in my head to go over and wake Kendall up and tell him I was too sick to go on. I'd tell him I wanted to take him up on that business of going to Canada in his car, and I knew he'd argue a little but not much, because if a guy was that far gone, there wasn't much use in trying to use him. So he'd let me do it, and I'd go there, and in a few days someone from The Man would show up and...

But I couldn't get that drunk. It would have been too easy, and there was still a little hope left in me.

I had to go on waiting and hoping, losing more of the little that was left of myself.

It didn't seem possible that I'd slipped so far, that so much had gone wrong in such a short length of time. I guess I'd been walking on the edge of a cliff for a long time, and it didn't take a very big breeze to start me sliding.

It was almost a relief to slide.

Well...

I got through the week. Sunday came again, and I kind of wanted to go to church and see Mrs. Summers again but I couldn't bring myself to do it. I got to thinking *why* about her—why I wanted to please her and make her face light up—and all I could think of was that I might be trying to pull something on her like I had on Mrs. Fields.

I spent almost the whole day at the bakery; not just my shift but the day. I was actually there longer than Kendall was, and you had to go some to beat him.

Finally, though, it was ten o'clock, and I hadn't done anything but loaf for a couple of hours. So when he suggested knocking off, I didn't have any excuse for staying.

I showered and changed clothes. We walked home together.

He said I was doing fine. "I've been able to turn in a very good report on you, Mr. Bigelow," he said.

"Swell," I said.

"Studies going satisfactorily? Nothing I can help you with? After all, we mustn't lose sight of the fact that your job is only a means to an end. If it interferes with your school—the reason for your being here—why—"

"I understand," I said.

We said good night and I turned in.

I woke up a couple of hours later when Fay crawled into bed with me.

She'd taken off her nightgown, and she snuggled up close to me, warm and soft and sweet-smelling.

A little moonlight sifted past the edge of the window shades. It fell across the pillows, and I could see into her eyes. And they didn't tell me a thing, as they should have. And because they didn't, they told me a lot.

I knew she was ready to spring it.

"Carl—" she said. "I—I've got something to tell you."

"Well?"

"It's about Jake. H-he—he's going to go back to jail until after the trial."

My guts sank into my stomach like a fist. Then a little laugh came out of me and I said, "You're kidding."

She rolled her head on the pillows. "It's the truth, honey, if he's telling me the truth. Is it—is it bad?"

"Bad," I said. "Is it bad!"

"I don't mean he's going right away, honey. Tonight's the first time he's mentioned it, and the way he hates jail it'll probably take him a week to work himself up—"

"But," I said, "what—why is he doing it?"

"Gosh, I just don't know, honey."

"You told me he couldn't take jail. You told me he'd never go back. He knew it wouldn't change a damned thing."

"You told me that, too, honey. Remember?" She squirmed lazily against the sheets. "Scratch my back, will you, baby? You know. Down low there."

I didn't scratch it. If I'd got a grip on her hide right then, I'd have pulled it off of her.

"Fay," I said. "Look at me."

"Mmmm?" She tilted her head and looked. "Like this, Carl?"

192

"Jake's been getting his nerve back. He's in a lot better shape than he was when I came here. Why this sudden notion to go back to jail?"

"I told you, honey, I don't know. It doesn't make sense."

"You think he means it?"

"I'm pretty sure he means it. Once he gets an idea in his head, like he did about you, you know, he never lets go."

"I see," I said.

"Is it ba—we can do it, now, can't we Carl? Let's kill him now and get it over with. The quicker it's done the sooner we can be together. I know you'd probably rather go on like this as long as you can, but—"

"Why?" I said. "Why do you think I'd rather?"

"Well, you would, wouldn't you? You're having a good time. You and your dear sweet little—t-trashy little—"

I said: "What the hell are you talking about?"

"Never mind. The point is I'm not going to go on like this any longer. Even if you do want to."

She wouldn't come all the way out with what was eating on her, and anyway I already knew. It would only lead to a brawl, and things were bad enough as they were.

"I'll tell you why I'd rather wait," I said. "I was told to. And the guy who told me wasn't talking to exercise his lungs."

"W-what do—" Her eyes shifted nervously. "I don't see what difference it makes if—"

"I told you. I spelled it out for you."

"Well, it doesn't make any difference! I don't care what anyone says. We can do it now just as well as not."

"All right. It doesn't make any difference," I said. "You said it doesn't, so that settles that."

She looked at me sullenly. I reached across her to the reading stand and got a cigarette lighted.

I let the match burn until the flame was almost to my finger tips. Then I dropped it, squarely between her breasts.

"*Oooof!*" She slapped and brushed at the match, stifling the instinctive scream into a gasp. "Y-you!" she whispered. "W-why did you—?"

"That's the way acid feels," I said. "Just a little like that. I imagine they'd start there and work up."

"B-but I—I haven't—"

"You're in with me. If I get it, you get it. Only you'd be a lot more interesting to work on."

That was wrong, to throw that kind of scare into her. I shouldn't make her think she had nothing to lose by pulling a doublecross. But...well, you see? For all I knew, she was already pulling one. Or on the point of doing it. And if I could make her see what it would cost her...

"You're sure about it?" I said. "You didn't misunderstand him, Fay? If you did, you'd better tell me."

"I—I—" She hesitated. "W-well, maybe I—"

"No lies. If that's the way it is I've got to know."

Her head moved shakily. "T-that's the way it is."

"I see," I said.

"I—I'll talk to him, Carl! I'll m-make him—he'll listen to me. I'll try to make him change his mind."

"You talk him into it," I said. "Then you try to talk him out of it. Huh-uh, baby. You're not that good."

"B-but I—what makes you think I—?"

"Don't kid me," I said. "How was it supposed to be, anyway? Jake's a nice boy, so they give him plenty of privileges in the jug, huh? He'll be safe and you can go right on seeing each other, and he won't be missing a thing. Is that it?"

She bit her lip. "M-maybe he doesn't mean it, Carl. Maybe he knows I didn't intend to—"

"Maybe," I nodded. "Maybe a couple of times. But like you said he's got the idea, and he doesn't let go of his ideas."

"B-but if...Oh, Carl, honey! W-what will they—?"

"Nothing," I said, and I lay down again and pulled her into my arms. "I'll straighten it out. We should have waited, but as long as we can't—"

"You're sure it'll be all right? You're sure, Carl?"

"I'm sure," I lied. "I'll fix it up. After all, Jake could have got the idea by himself. They won't know that he didn't."

She sighed and relaxed a little. I kept on soothing her, telling her it would be all right, and after a while I got rid of her. She slipped back to her room.

I uncorked a pint I had, and sat on the edge of the bed drinking. It was around daylight when I went to sleep.

...I called The Man from a booth in that quiet little bar I'd found. He answered right away, and the first thing he asked me was where I was calling from. He said that was good, splendid, when I told him. And, dammit, it *was;* it was as good as I could do. So many drunks phone from bars that no one pays any attention to the calls.

But I knew he didn't think it was good. He didn't think I should be calling him at all.

He told me he'd call me back. I hung up and had a couple of drinks while he went to another phone.

"All right, Charlie—" his voice came over the wire again. "What's on your mind?"

"Our—that merchandise," I said. "It looks like it was going off the market. We'll have to act fast to get it."

"I don't understand," he said.

"You'd better speak plainly. I hardly think that our conversation can be completely camouflaged and comprehensible at the same time."

"All right," I said. "Jake's talking about going to jail until after the trial. I'm not sure whether he means it or not, but I thought I'd better not take any chances."

"You want to do it now, then. Soon."

"Well"—I hesitated—"I can't do it after he's in jail."

"That isn't what we agreed on, Charlie."

"I know," I said, "but I—"

"You said he'd been talking about it. To whom?"

"To Mrs. Winroy."

"I see. And does she still have your fullest confidence, Charlie? You'll recall, I believe, that I had some few small doubts about her myself."

"I think she's telling the truth," I said.

"Why does she say Jake's going to jail?"

"She doesn't say. Jake didn't tell her."

"Strange." He paused. "I find that slightly puzzling."

"Look," I said. "I know it doesn't seem right, but Jake's half-way off his rocker! He's running around in circles."

"A moment, please. Am I wrong or wasn't it Mrs. Winroy's job to keep Jake available? You were very sure she could do that, weren't you? And now the opposite has happened."

"Yes, sir," I said.

"Why, Charlie?"

"I don't know," I said. "I don't know whether he's really going to do it."

He was silent for a long time. I'd about decided he'd hung up. Then, he laughed softly and said:

"You do whatever you think is necessary, Charlie. As soon as you think it's necessary."

"I know how you feel," I said. "I haven't been here very long, and...I know it would look better if I could have waited."

"Yes. And there's the matter of publicity, having the story kept alive for weeks. Or perhaps you've forgotten that in the press of your other affairs?"

"Look," I said. "Is it all right or not? I want to know."

He didn't answer me.

That time he *had* hung up.

I picked up my books off the bar and went on to school. Cursing Fay, but not putting much heart into it. It was my fault for bringing her into the deal.

The Man hadn't wanted her in. If she hadn't been in and Jake had got this jail idea on his own, I wouldn't have been held responsible. As it was...

Well, a lot depended on how things worked out. If it all went off all right they'd go easy on me. No money, of course. Or, if I had the guts and was stupid enough to ask for money, a few bills and a beating. They'd leave me here—that would be my payoff. I'd be left here to rot, with no dough but the little I had and no way I could get any more. Just barely scraping by on some cheap job, as long as I could hold a job and then...

The Man would get a kick out of that. Hell—*the* hell—he knew you didn't have to dig for it, too.

And if the job didn't go right...

It didn't make much difference. I couldn't win.

19

It was Sunday when Fay had given me the bad news. We set Jake up for Thursday night.

So there were four days there, between the first thing and the second. Four whole days. But it didn't seem that long. It seemed like I'd walked out of the bar, after I'd talked to The Man, and stepped straight into Thursday night.

I was through, washed up. I wasn't living; I was just going through the motions.

Living is remembering, I guess. If you've lost interest, if everything is that same shade of gray, the kind you see when you look into light with your eyes closed, if nothing seems worth storing away, either as bad or good, reward or retribution, then you may keep going for a while. But you don't live. And you don't remember.

I went to school. I worked. I ate and slept. And drank. And . . . Yes, and Ruthie. I talked to her a few times on the way to and from school. I remembered—yes, I *did* remember her. I remember wondering what would become of her. Wishing I could help her some way.

But aside from Ruthie, nothing.

Except for the few minutes I was with her, I moved straight from Monday into Thursday. Thursday night at eight o'clock.

I snapped out of it then, and came back to life. You have to at a time like that whether you want to or not.

It was a slow night on the job, one of the slowest in the week. I was all caught up on my work, and no one had any reason to come into the stockroom.

I stood in the outer storeroom with the light turned off, watching the other side of the street.

Fay went by, right on the dot at eight.

I studied my watch, waiting. At eight-fifteen, Jake went by.

I unlocked the door and stepped out.

It was a good dark night. He was moving in a beeline for the house, not looking to right or left.

I sauntered down the side of the street the bakery was on, until he'd passed the intersection. Then I crossed over and followed him, walking faster because he'd got quite a way ahead of me.

I was about fifty feet behind him when he started across the parallel street to the house. Just about the right distance, allowing for the time he needed to open the gate. He fumbled with it, unable to find the catch, and I slowed down to where I was barely moving. At last he got it open, and I...

I froze in my tracks.

He—this guy—was a drunk, I found out later. He'd come out of that little bar catercornered to the house and wandered across the road, and I don't know how the hell he'd managed it but somehow he'd fallen over inside the fence. He was lying there when Jake came along, inside and up against the fence. As Jake opened the gate, he rose up and sort of staggered toward him. And Jake let out a yell.

And that front yard was suddenly as bright as day.

Two big floodlights struck it from the vacant lots on each side of the house. Cops—deputy sheriffs, rather—swarmed up from everywhere.

I stood frozen for a second, unable to move. Then I turned around and started walking back to the bakery.

I'd gotten almost to the corner when I heard a yell from the sheriff rising above the other yells. *"Wait a minute, dang it! This ain't the right—"*

I kept right on going, and I was crossing the street to the bakery before the shout came. *"You there! Halt!"*

I didn't halt. What the hell? He was almost two blocks away. How should I know he was hollering at me?

I went right on into the bakery, locking the door behind me. I went into the main stockroom, closed the connecting door, and sat down at my work table.

I picked up the batch cards for the night, and began checking them off against my perpetual inventory.

Someone was banging on that outside door. I stayed where I was. What the hell again? I couldn't let anyone in that door this time of night. Why, it might be a robber, someone trying to steal a sack of flour!

The banging stopped. I grinned to myself, flipping through the cards. I was alive again. I'd have laid down for them, but since I couldn't do that, I'd make them lay me.

The door to the baking room slammed open. Kendall and the sheriff and a deputy came in, the sheriff in the lead.

I stood up. I went toward him, holding out my hand.

"Why, how are you, sheriff?" I said. "How is Mrs. Sum—"

He swung his hand, knocking mine aside so hard that it almost spun me around. His fingers knotted in my shirt, and he yanked me clean off the floor. He shook me like a dog shakes a rat. If ever I saw murder in a mug it was his.

"You snotty little punk!" He shook and swung me with one hand and began slapping me with the other. "Think you're cute, huh? Think it's smart to go around so danged nice an' lovey-dovey, gettin' people to trust you and then—"

I didn't blame him for being sore. I guess no one can ever be as sore at you as the guy who's liked and trusted you. But that hand of his was as hard as a rock, and Kendall couldn't get past the deputy to stop him like he was trying to do.

I passed out.

20

I wasn't out very long, I guess, but it was long enough for Dr. Dodson to get there. I came to, stretched out on the floor with my head on some flour sacking and the doc bent over me.

"How are you feeling, son?" he said. "Any pain?"

"Of course, he's in pain!" Kendall snapped. "This—this creature beat him within an inch of his life!"

"Now, wait a minute, dang it! I didn't—"

"Shut up, Summers. How about it, son?"

"I—I feel all right," I said. "Just kind of dizzy, and—" I coughed and began to choke. He raised my shoulders quickly, and I bent over, choking and coughing, and blood spilled down on the floor in a little pool.

He took the handkerchief out of his breast pocket and wiped my mouth with it. He lowered me back to the floor again, and stood up, staring at the sheriff.

The sheriff looked back at him, sullen and sheepish.

"Kinda lost my temper," he mumbled. "Reckon you would've, too, doc, if you'd been in my place. He was all set t'do Winroy in, just like the note said he'd be, and then this danged drunk gets in the way an' he comes saunterin' back here, just as pretty as you please, and—"

"You know," the doctor cut in, quietly. "You know something, Summers? If I had a gun I think I'd blow that fat head of yours right off your shoulders."

The sheriff's mouth dropped open. He looked stunned, and sort of sick. "Now, now looky here," he stammered. "This— you don't know who this fella is! He's Charlie Bigger, Little Bigger, they call him. He's a killer, an'—"

"He is, eh? But you took care of him, didn't you?"

"You want to know what happened or not?" Sheriff Summers' face turned a few shades redder. "He—"

"I'll tell you what happened," Kendall spoke up coldly. "Carl stepped out for a little walk, as he has my permission to do when his work is caught up. In fact, I've encouraged him to do it since his illness. He was in the vicinity of the Winroy house when this ruckus broke out, and having something better to do with his time than gawk and gape at matters which did not concern him—"

"The heck they didn't concern him! How come the note said he—"

"—he came back here," said Kendall. "A few minutes later, Summers came storming into the bakery with this—uh— hireling and started babbling some nonsense about Carl's having tried to murder someone and failing to stop when he was ordered to. Then he rushed in here and attacked him, beat him into unconsciousness. I've never seen such savagely inexcusable brutality in my life, Dod!"

"I see," the doctor nodded, and turned to the sheriff. "Well?"

Sheriff Summers' lips came together in a thin hard line. "Never mind," he grunted. "You want it that way, you have it that way. I'm takin' him to jail."

"On what charge? Taking a walk?"

"Attempted murder, that's what!"

"And what are your grounds for such a charge?"

"I already told—!" The sheriff broke off, his head lowered like a mad bull. "Never you mind. I'm takin' him in."

He started toward me, the deputy hanging back like he was pretty unhappy, and Kendall and the doc stepped in his way. In about another ten seconds, I think he'd have had a knockdown drag-out fight on his hands. And there wasn't any sense in that, so I got up.

I felt all right, everything considered. Just a little smaller and weaker than I had felt.

"I'll go," I said.

"We can settle it; you don't need to go," the doctor said, and Kendall added, "No, he certainly does *not* need to!"

"I'd rather go," I said. "Sheriff Summers and his wife have been very nice to me. I'm sure he wouldn't be doing this if he didn't think it was necessary."

There was some more argument from Dodson and Kendall, but I went. We all went.

We got to the courthouse just as the county attorney was going up the steps, and the deputy took us into the c.a.'s office while he and the sheriff stood in the corridor talking.

The sheriff had his back to the door, but the county attorney was facing it, and he looked weary and disgusted. All the time the sheriff was talking, he just stood there with his hands shoved into his pockets, frowning and shaking his head.

Finally, they came inside, and he and the sheriff started to ask a question at the same time. They both stopped, one waiting for the other, then they started again, both at once. They did that about three times, and the doctor let out a snort and Kendall sort of half smiled. The county attorney grimaced and leaned back in his chair.

"All right, Bill," he sighed. "It's your headache, anyway."

Sheriff Summers turned to me.

"What's your name? Your right name?"

"You know what it is, sheriff," I said.

"It's Charlie Bigger, ain't it? You're Little Charlie Bigger."

"Suppose I said, yes," I said. "Then what? I'd like to accommodate you, sheriff, but I don't see how that would help."

"I asked you what your—!" He broke off as the county attorney caught his eyes. "All right," he grunted. "What was you doin' sneaking along behind Jake Winroy tonight?"

"I wasn't sneaking anywhere. I was walking."

"You always go for a walk at that time o'night?"

"Not always. Often. It's a slack time for me."

"How come you was walkin' toward the Winroy place instead of the other way?"

"These work clothes. Naturally, I wouldn't want to walk up toward the business district."

"I got a note about you. It had you right down to a *t*. Said you was gonna do just what you—what you tried to do."

"What was that?" I said.

"You know what. Kill Jake Winroy!"

"Kill him?" I said. "Why, I didn't try to kill him, sheriff."

"You would have! If that danged drunk—"

Dr. Dodson let out another snort. "Anonymous notes! What next?"

"He was there, wasn't he?" The sheriff whirled on him. "How come I got that note if—"

"I believe it has been established," the county attorney sighed, "that he is in that vicinity almost every night at approximately that time."

"But Winroy ain't! It ain't been established how I—"

Kendall cleared his throat. "Since you seem to be unwilling to accept the note as the work of some crank who has observed Mr. Bigelow's movements and who profited by an unfortunate but by no means extraordinary coincidence—"

"It's too danged extraordinary for me!"

"As I was saying, then, the note can only be explained in one way. This shrewd and crafty killer"—he smiled apologetically at me—"the most elusive, close-mouthed criminal in the country, went around town confiding his plans...Something wrong, sheriff?"

"I didn't say he done that! I—I—"

"I see. It's your theory, then, that he wrote you—or I believe it was printed, wasn't it?—he sent you the note himself. So that you'd be on hand to apprehend him."

Doc Dodson burst out laughing. The county attorney tried not to laugh, but he couldn't quite hold it back.

"Well," he said, bringing his hands down on the desk. "Bill, I think the best thing we can do is—"

"Now, wait a minute! He could have had someone workin' with him! They could've given him away!"

"Oh, come now." Kendall shook his head. "He's a stranger here. I live with him and work with him, and I can assure you he has no intimates aside from me. But perhaps that's what you had in mind, sheriff? You think I was involved in this matter."

"I didn't say so, did I?" The sheriff glared at him helplessly. "I—anyway, that ain't all I got on him. I got a wire from the kin of some folks he used to live with. They said he swindled and abused these old people, and—"

"I believe you got two other wires about me, also," I said. "From a chief of police and a county judge. What did they say about me?"

"I—well—why'd you run away tonight?"

"I didn't do any running, sheriff."

"Why didn't you stop when I hollered? You heard me."

"I heard someone, but they were a couple of blocks away. I didn't know they were hollering at me."

"Well—uh—why—?"

He paused, trying to think of something else to ask me. He wet his lips, hesitating. He slanted a glance at Kendall and Dodson and the county attorney, and in his mind's eye, I guess, he was also looking at his wife, wondering how he was going to explain and excuse himself to her.

The county attorney yawned and massaged his eyes. "Well," he said, "I suppose we'll have an army of city cops moving in on us now. Ordering us around and telling us how to run our business like they did last time."

"Now, I—I—" The sheriff gulped. "I don't reckon we will. My boys ain't letting out anything."

"He'd probably like that," said Dr. Dodson. "Likes to get his picture in the papers. If I didn't think you'd suffer enough without it, I'd file a complaint against you with the county commissioners."

"You will, hey?" The sheriff jumped to his feet. "Hop right to it! Go ahead and see if I give a dang."

"We'll see," Dodson nodded, grimly. "Meanwhile, I'm going to take this boy to my clinic and put him to bed."

"You are, huh? He ain't going anywhere."

"Very well. He needs rest and medical attention. I've said so. These gentlemen are my witnesses. And I'll tell you something, Summers—" He slammed on his hat. "Don't be too surprised if you find them testifying against you on a charge of murder by criminal neglect."

"Pshaw." The sheriff's eyes wavered. "How come he gets around like he's been doin' if he's so sick? You can't tell me—"

"I could but I doubt that you'd understand... Coming, Phil?"

Well...

I went to the clinic.

The doctor checked me over from head to foot, shaking his head and grunting now and then in a kind of baffled way. Then he gave me a shot glass of some yellowish stuff, and three hypodermic injections, one in each hip and the other right over my heart; and I went to sleep.

But Sheriff Summers still hadn't given up. He posted a deputy on my door at the clinic that night. And the next morning, around eleven, he came in and threw some more questions at me.

He didn't look like he'd got much sleep. I'd have bet dough that Mrs. Summers had eaten him out to a fare-you-well.

He was still at it, going through the motions of playing cop, when Kendall showed up. Kendall spoke to him pleasantly. He suggested that they take a little walk, and they left together.

I grinned and lighted a cigarette. Kendall was starting to earn his money, if he hadn't already earned it. It was the first real chance he'd had to get the sheriff alone.

The next thing he'd do, now...

The rest and the stuff the doctor had given me seemed to have perked me up quite a bit. And I guess a guy always fights best just before he's through fighting. I didn't think I could beat The Man—no one ever beat The Man—but I figured I could give him plenty of trouble. It might be a year or two before he could hunt me down, and if I could hold out that long...well. Maybe I could find the place or the thing or whatever it was I'd always been looking for.

I had almost five hundred dollars—more in the bank in Arizona, but I might as well forget about that. With five hundred bucks and a good car—and there was a drop in Philly where I could turn that car fast for another one—well, it was worth a try. I couldn't lose anything.

...It was almost two o'clock when Kendall came back. And I was sure of what he was going to say, but he led into it so gradually that I almost got unsure.

Mrs. Winroy had gone to New York, he said. Her sister had taken sick and she'd had to leave suddenly.

"Poor woman. I've never seen her quite so agitated."

"That's too bad," I said, wanting to laugh so bad it hurt me. She'd probably worry herself to death before they could get to her. "When is she coming back?"

"She wasn't able to say. I gathered, however, that it might be quite some time."

"Well," I said, "that's certainly too bad."

"Yes. Particularly with nothing better than Winroy to depend on. I wanted to talk to him — straighten out our accounts since Mrs. Winroy isn't available, but Ruthie hasn't seen anything of him since lunchtime and he's not at his shop. I suppose, now that the last restraining influence is gone, he intends to get drunk and stay drunk."

I nodded. And waited. He went on.

"An awkward situation. Poor Ruthie; it's really a tragedy in her case. There's no other place she can get a job, and, with Mrs. Winroy gone indefinitely, she can't stay there. I'd like to help her, but — uh — a man my age, giving financial assistance to a girl who obviously could not repay it...I'm afraid it would do her more harm than good."

"She's dropping out of school?"

"I'm afraid there's no alternative. She seems to be bearing up very well, I'm happy to say."

"Well," I said. "It looks like we — like you'll have to be finding another place to live."

"Uh, yes. Yes, I suppose I will. Uh — er — incidentally,

Mr. Bigelow, the sheriff is satisfied to—uh—abandon this Winroy matter. I've brought your clothes from the bakery, your pay to date also since it seemed doubtful in view of your health, and—uh—the situation in general—that you would care to continue there."

"I see," I said. "I understand."

"About Sheriff Summers, Mr. Bigelow. His attitude is by no means as compromising as I would like to have it. I suspect that he would need only the slightest pretext, if any, to—uh—cause you serious embarrassment."

I thought it over; rather I appeared to be thinking it over. I laughed, kind of hurt, and said, "It looks like I'm out of luck all the way around, Mr. Kendall. No place to live. No job. The sheriff all set to make trouble. The—I don't suppose the college will be exactly happy to have me around either."

"Well—uh—as a matter of fact—"

"It's all right," I said. "I don't blame them a bit."

He shook his head sympathetically, clucking his tongue a few times. Then he looked up sharply, eyes sparkling, and came out with it. As though it had just then popped into his mind.

"Mr. Bigelow! This may turn out to be a stroke of good fortune in disguise! You can go up to my place in Canada for a few months, use the time for studying and rebuilding your health. Then, when all this business is forgotten—"

"Gosh," I said. "You mean you'd still be willing to—?"

"Certainly, I would! Now, most of all. Of course, we'll have to see what the doctor has to say about you, but—"

…The doctor didn't like it much. He fussed quite a bit,

particularly when he found out that I wanted to leave town that day. But Kendall fussed right back, calling him a pessimist and so on. Then he took him to one side, explaining, I guess, that I didn't have much choice about leaving. So...

We drove to the house in Kendall's car, me driving since he didn't like to. He asked me if I'd mind driving Ruthie to her folks' farm on my way, and I said I wouldn't mind at all.

I stopped in front of the house, and we stood at the side of the car for a few minutes, talking but not getting much said.

"By the way, Mr. Bigelow," he said, hesitantly, "I know I've seemed inexcusably dictatorial during our all too brief acquaintance. I'm sure there must have been a great many times when you must have felt like telling me to mind my own business."

"Oh, no," I said. "Not at all, Mr. Kendall."

"Oh, yes." He smiled at me. "And I'm afraid my reasons were extremely selfish ones. Do you believe in immortality, Mr. Bigelow? In the broadest sense of the word, that is? Well, let me simply say then that I seem to have done almost none of the many things which I had planned on doing in this tearful vale. They are still there in me, waiting to be done, yet the span of time for their doing has been exhausted. I... But listen to me, will you?" He chuckled embarrassedly, his eyes blinking behind their glasses. "I didn't think myself capable of such absurd poeticism!"

"That's all right," I said, slowly, and a kind of chill crept over me. "What do you mean your span—"

I was looking straight into him, through him and out the other side, and all I could see was a prim, fussy old guy. That was all I could see, because that was all there was to see. *He wasn't working for The Man. He never had been.*

"...so little time, Mr. Bigelow. None to waste on preliminaries. Everything that could be done for you had to be done quickly."

"Why didn't you tell me?" I said. "For Christ's sake, why—"

"Tsk, tsk, Mr. Bigelow. Fret you with the irremediable? Place yet another boulder in your already rocky path? There is nothing to be done about it. I am dying and that is that."

"But I...if you'd only told me!"

"I only tell you now because it is unavoidable. As I have indicated in the past, I am not exactly a pauper. I wanted you to be in a position to understand when you heard from my attorneys."

I couldn't say anything. I couldn't even see the way my eyes were stinging and burning. Then he grabbed my hand and shook it, and his grip almost made me holler.

"Dignity, Mr. Bigelow! I insist on it. If you must be mawkish, at least wait until I...I—"

He let go of me, and when my eyes cleared he was gone.

I opened the gate to the yard, wondering how I could have been so wrong. But there really wasn't much to wonder about. I'd picked him because I didn't want to pick the logical person. The person who could do everything he could, and who had a lot better reason for doing it...Ruthie.

I wasn't particularly quiet going into the house, so I guess she heard me, even if she didn't let on. The drapes to the living room were pulled back and her bedroom door was open, and I stood watching her, braced against the end of the bedstead, as she pulled on her clothes.

214

I looked her over, a little at a time, as though she wasn't one thing but many, as though she wasn't one woman but a thousand, all women. And then my eyes settled on that little foot with its little ankle, and everything else seemed to disappear. And I thought:

"Well, how could I? How can you admit you're screwing yourself?"

She put on her brassiere and her slip before she took notice of me. She let out a gasp and said, "Oh, C-Carl! I didn't—"

"About ready?" I said. "I'll drive you out to your folks."

"C-Carl, I—I—"

She came toward me, slowly, rocking on her crutch. "I want to go with you, Carl! I don't care what you've—I don't care about anything! Just so I can be with you."

"Yeah," I said. "I know. You were always afraid I'd go away, weren't you? You were willing to do anything you could to keep me here. Help me with the school, sleep with me...be Johnny-on-the-spot if I needed you for anything. And you couldn't leave either, could you, Ruthie? You couldn't lose your job."

"Take me, Carl! You've got to take me with you!"

I wasn't sure yet. So I said, "Well, go on and get ready. We'll see."

Then, I went upstairs to my room.

I packed my two suitcases. I turned back a corner of the carpet and picked up a carbon copy of the note I'd sent to the sheriff.

For, naturally, I had sent the note. I'd meant to tell Ruthie about the carbon afterwards so that she could take credit for the tip and claim the rewards.

I hadn't had anything to lose, as I saw it. I couldn't help myself, so I'd tried to help her. The person who might wind up as I had if she didn't have help.

I hesitated a moment, turning the slip of paper around in my fingers. But it was no good now. They'd muffed their chance to catch me in the act of attempting to kill Jake Winroy, and I figured there was at least one damned good reason why they'd never get another one.

I figured that way, but I wanted to make sure. I burned the carbon in an ashtray, and crossed the hall to Jake's room.

I stood at the side of his bed, looking down. At him and the note Ruthie had written.

It was stupid; no one would believe that Jake had tried to attack her and she'd done it in self-defense. But, well, I could understand. The whole setup had been falling apart. Ruthie had to do it fast if at all. And I guess if a person is willing to do a thing like that, then he's stupid to begin with and it's bound to crop out on him sooner or later.

It was all wrong. The Man wouldn't like it. And getting me for him wouldn't help her any. She had to latch on to me now, of course; and you get stupider and stupider the farther you go. But excuses didn't cut any ice with The Man. He picked you because you were stupid; he *made* you stupid, you might say. But if you slipped up, *you* did it. And you got what The Man gave people who slipped.

It was done, though, and me, I was done, too. So nothing

mattered now but to let her go on hoping. As long as she could hope...

I took one last look at Jake before I left the room. Ruthie had almost sawed his throat out with one of his own razors. Scared, you know, and scared not to. Angry because she was scared. It looked a lot like the job I'd done on Fruit Jar.

21

I'd never seen the place, just the road that led up to it; and I'd only seen that the one time years before when that writer had driven me by on the way to the train. But I didn't have any trouble finding it again. The road was grown high with weeds, and in some places long vines had spread across it from the bare-branched trees on either side.

The road sloped up from the Vermont highway, then down again, so that unless you were right there, right on top of them, you couldn't see the house and the farm buildings. Ruth looked at me pretty puzzled a time or two, but she didn't ask any questions. I ran the car into the garage and closed the doors, and we walked back toward the house.

There was a sign fastened to the gate. It said:

BEWARE OF WILD GOATS
"The Way of the Trespasser is Hard"

And there was a typewritten notice tacked to the back door:

Departed for parts unknown. Will supply
forwarding address, if, when, and as soon as possible.

The door was unlocked. We went in.

I looked all through the house, by myself mostly because the stairs were steep and narrow and Ruthie couldn't have got around so good. I went through room after room, and he wasn't there, of course, no one was there, and everything was covered with dust but everything was in order. All the rooms were in order but one, a little tiny one way off by itself on the second floor. And except for the way the typewriter was ripped apart, even that one had a kind of order about it.

The furniture was all pushed back against the wall, and there was nothing in the bookcases but the covers of books. The pages of them and God knows how many other pages—typewritten ones that hadn't been made into books—had been torn up like confetti. And the confetti was stacked in little piles all over the floor. Arranged into letters and words:

And the Lord World so loved the god that It gave him Its only begotten son, and thenceforth He was driven from the Garden and Judas wept, saying, Verily I abominate onions yet I can never refuse them.

I kicked the piles of paper apart, and went downstairs.
We moved in, and stayed.
There was case after case of canned goods in the cellar. There

was a drum of coal oil for the lamps and the two stoves. There was a water well with an inside pump at the sink. There wasn't any electricity or telephone or radio or anything like that; we were shut off from everything, as though we were in another world. But we had everything else, and ourselves. So we stayed.

The days drifted by, and I wondered what she was waiting for. And there was nothing to do...except what could be done with ourselves. And I seemed to be shrinking more and more, getting weaker and littler while she got stronger and bigger. And I began to think maybe she was going to do it that way.

Some nights, afterwards, when I wasn't too weak and sick to do it, I'd stand at the window, staring out at the fields with their jungle of weeds and vines. The wind rippled through them, making them sway and wiggle and squirm. And there was a howling and a shrieking in my ears—but after a while it went away. Everywhere, everywhere I looked, the jungle swayed and wiggled and squirmed. It shook that thing at me. There was something sort of hypnotic about it, and I'd still be weak and sick, but I wouldn't notice it. There wouldn't be a thing in my mind but that thing, and I'd wake her up again. And then it was like I was running a race, I was trying to get to something, get something, before the howling came back. Because when I heard that I had to stop.

But all I ever got was that thing. Not the other, whatever the other was.

The goats always won.

22

The days drifted by, and she knew that I knew, of course, but we never talked about it. We never talked about anything much because we were cut off from everything, and after a while everything was said that we could say and it would have been like talking to yourself. So we talked less and less, and pretty soon we were hardly talking at all. And then we *weren't* talking at all. Just grunting and gesturing and pointing at things.

It was like we'd never known how to talk.

It began to get pretty cold, so we shut off all the upstairs rooms and stayed downstairs. And it got colder and we shut off all the rooms but the living room and the kitchen. And it got colder and we shut off all the rooms but the kitchen. We lived there, never more than a few feet away from each other. It was always right close by, that thing was, and outside... it was out there too. It seemed to edge in closer and closer, from all sides, and there was no way to get away from it. And I didn't want to get away. I kept getting weaker and littler, but I couldn't stop. There was nothing else to think about, so I kept taking that thing. I'd go for it fast, trying to win the race against the goats. And I never did, but I kept on trying. I had to.

Afterwards, when the howling began to get so bad I couldn't stand it, I'd go outside looking for the goats. I'd go running and screaming and clawing my way through the fields, wanting to get my hands on just one of them. And I never did, of course, because the fields weren't really the place to find the goats.

23

I couldn't eat much of anything. The basement was loaded with food and whiskey, but I had a hard time getting any down. I'd eaten less and less ever since that first day when I'd raised up the trap door that was set flush with the kitchen floor and gone down the steep narrow steps.

I'd gone down them, taking a lantern with me, and I'd looked all along the shelves, packed tight with bottles and packages and canned goods. I'd circled around the room, looking, and I came to a sort of setback in the walls—a doorless closet, kind of. And the entrance to it was blocked off, stacked almost to the ceiling with empty bottles.

I wondered why in hell they'd been dumped there instead of outside, because it would be stupid of a guy to drink the stuff upstairs, where he naturally would drink it, and then bring the bottles back down here. As long as he was up there, why hadn't he...?

24

I said we never talked, but we did. We talked all the time to the goats. I talked to them while she slept and she talked to them while I slept. Or maybe it was the other way around. Anyway, I did my share of talking.

I said we lived in the one room, but we didn't. We lived in all the rooms, but they were all the same. And wherever we were the goats were always there. I couldn't ever catch them but I knew they were there. They'd come up out of the fields and moved in with us, and sometimes I'd almost get my hands on them but they always got away. She'd get in my way before I could grab them.

I thought and I thought about it, and finally I knew how it must be. They'd been there all along. Right there, hiding inside of her. So it wasn't any wonder I could never win the race.

I knew they were in her, where else could they be, but I had to make sure. And I couldn't.

I couldn't touch her. She didn't sleep with me any more. She ate a lot, enough for two people, and sometimes in the morning she vomited...

It was right after the vomiting started that she began walking. I mean, really walking, not using the crutch.

She'd tuck her dress up around her waist, so that it wouldn't be in the way, and walk back and forth on one knee and that little foot. She got to where she could walk pretty good. She'd hold her good foot up behind her with one hand, making a stump out of the knee. It came just about even, then, with that little baby foot and she could get around pretty fast.

She'd walk for an hour at a time with her dress tucked up and everything she had showing, but you'd never have known I was there from the way she acted. She...

Hell, she talked to me. She explained to me. We'd been talking all the time, and not to the goats either, because of course there weren't any goats, and...

She walked on the little foot, exercising the goats. And at night they sat on my chest howling.

25

I stayed in the basement as much as I could. She couldn't get me down there. She wasn't good enough on that little foot and knee to come down the stairs. And somehow I had to hang on.

The last race was over, and I'd lost them all, but still I hung on. I seemed to be right on the point of finding something... of finding out something. And until I did I couldn't leave.

I found out one evening when I was coming up out of the basement. I came even with the floor and turned sideways on the steps, putting down the stuff I'd brought up. And I'd brought a pretty big load because I didn't want to come up any more often than I had to; and I was kind of dizzy. I leaned my arms on the floor, steadying myself. And then my eyes cleared, and there was the little foot and leg right in front of me. Braced.

The axe flashed. My hand, my right hand, jumped and kind of leaped away from me, sliced off clean. And she swung again and all my left hand was gone but the thumb. She moved in closer, raising the axe for another swing...

And so, at last, I knew.

26

Back there. Back to the place I'd come from. And, hell, I'd never been wanted there to begin with.

"*... but where else, my friend? Where a more logical retreat in this tightening circle of frustration?*"

She was swinging wild. My right shoulder was hanging by a thread, and the spouting forearm dangled from it. And my scalp, my scalp and the left side of my face was dangling, and... and I didn't have a nose...or a chin...or...

I went over backwards, then down and down and down, turning so slowly in the air it seemed that I was hardly moving. I didn't know it when I hit the bottom. I was simply there, looking up as I'd been looking on the way down.

Then there was a slam and a click, and she was gone.

27

The darkness and myself. Everything else was gone. And the little that was left of me was going, faster and faster.

I began to crawl. I crawled and rolled and inched my way along; and I missed it the first time—the place I was looking for.

I circled the room twice before I found it, and there was hardly any of me then but it was enough. I crawled up over the pile of bottles, and went crashing down the other side.

And he was there, of course.

Death was there.

28

And he smelled good.

ABOUT THE AUTHOR

Jim Thompson (1906–1977), widely celebrated as America's "Dimestore Dostoevsky," was one of the most prolific crime-fiction writers of his generation. As a teenager, he sold his first story to *True Detective*, and he went on to write twenty-nine acclaimed novels. He also cowrote two original screenplays (for the Stanley Kubrick films *The Killing* and *Paths of Glory*). Several of his novels have been adapted into films, including the noir classics *The Killer Inside Me; After Dark, My Sweet;* and *The Grifters*.

...AND *NOW AND ON EARTH*

Mulholland Books also publishes Jim Thompson's *Now and on Earth*. Following is an excerpt from the novel's opening pages.

I

I got off at three-thirty, but it took me almost an hour to walk home. The factory is a mile off Pacific Boulevard, and we live a mile up the hill from Pacific. Or up the mountain, I should say. How they ever managed to pour concrete on those hill streets is beyond me. You can tie your shoelaces going up them without stooping.

Jo was across the street, playing with the minister's little girl. Watching for me, too, I guess. She came streaking across to my side, corn-yellow curls bobbing around her rose-and-white face. She hugged me around the knees and kissed my hand—something I don't like her to do, but can't stop.

She asked me how I liked my new job, and how much pay I was getting, and when payday was—all in one breath. I told her not to talk so loud out in public, that I wasn't getting as much as I had with the foundation, and that payday was Friday, I thought.

"Can I get a new hat then?"

"I guess so. If it's all right with Mother."

Jo frowned. "Mother won't let me have it. I know she won't.

She took Mack and Shannon downtown to buy 'em some new shoes, but she won't get me no hat."

" 'No hat'?"

"Any hat, I mean."

"Where'd she get the money to go shopping with? Didn't she pay the rent?"

"I guess not," Jo said.

"Oh, goddam!" I said. "Now, what the hell will we do? Well, what are you gaping for? Go on and play. Get away from me. Get out of my sight. Go on, go on!"

I reached out to shake her, but I caught myself and hugged her instead. I cannot stand anyone who is unkind to children — children, dogs, or old people. I don't know what is getting the matter with me that I would shake Jo. I don't know.

"Don't pay any attention to me, baby," I said. "You know I didn't mean anything."

Jo's smile came back. "You're just tired, that's all," she said. "You go in and lie down and you'll feel better."

I said I would, and she kissed my hand again and scurried back across the street.

Jo is nine — my oldest child.

2

I was tired, and I hurt. The lung I'd had collapsed during the winter seemed to be filled with molasses, and my piles were torturing me.

I hollered when I got inside the door, but no one answered so I supposed Mom was gone, too. I went in the bathroom and washed, and tried to do something about my piles, and washed again. No good. I went at it again, and I washed some more. And then I remembered that I'd already done the same thing about six times, so I stopped.

The refrigerator did have some ice-cubes in it. Nothing but ice-cubes, and some old celery, and a few grapefruit, and a stick of butter. But that was something. Mom has a hard time getting the trays out, and when she does she usually leaves them out. Roberta never puts any water in the trays. She'll take them out, remove all the cubes, and put them back without a drop of water. Jo and I are about the only ones in the house who always fill the trays and put them back where they belong. If it wasn't for us, we'd never have any ice.

God, listen to me rave! And about ice-cubes. I don't know what's getting into me.

While I was standing there drinking and scratching and

wondering about things in general, Mom came in from the bedroom. She'd been asleep, and she was still barefooted. Mom has varicose veins. She's always had them as far back as I can remember. Or—that's not true either. Her legs were never real good, but she didn't have those veins until I was nine years old. I remember how she got them.

It was about a week after Frankie, my younger sister, was born. Pop was down in Texas, trying to complete an oil well. We were existing in a shack deep down on Oklahoma City's West Main Street. A tough part of town in those days; I guess it still is.

Margaret—that's my older sister—and I were sort of living off the neighbors, and Mom wasn't eating much. So that left only Frankie to take care of. But she couldn't eat handouts, and Mom couldn't nurse her, and we only had fifty cents in the house.

Well, Margaret and I went down to the drugstore after a jar of malted milk, and on the way back a group of the neighborhood hoodlums chased us. And Margaret dropped the bottle. It was all wrapped up in that tough brown paper, and we didn't know it was broken until Mom unwrapped it.

No, she didn't scold or spank us—to the best of my recollection we never received a real spanking—she just sat there among the pillows, and something terrible happened to her face. And then she placed one starved hand over her eyes and her shoulders trembled and she cried.

I think an artist must have been peeking in the window that night, for years later I saw a painting of Mom. A painting of a woman in a torn gown, tangled black hair and thin hand concealing her face but not hiding—oh, Jesus, no! not hiding but pointing at—wretchedness and pain and hopelessness that were unspeakable. It was called *Despair*.

But the artist should have stayed for the sequel.

We got some newspapers and spread them out on the bed, and dumped the malt out on it. And then Marge and I and Mom began to pick the glass out of it. We picked and sorted and strained our eyes for an hour or more, and just when we had a few spoonfuls without any glass in it, Frankie woke up with one of those wild kicking fits which characterized her awakenings. She almost bounced us off the bed. Somehow we held on, keeping the glass from being re-mixed with the milk. But it didn't do any good. Frankie had only been limbering up for the main event. Her nightdress had gone up with the first kicks, and now her diaper slipped down....

Well, we threw the papers away and mopped up a little—it was so funny we all had to laugh—and Mom asked us what we thought we'd better do now. Marge, who was twelve, said she'd brought some chalk home from school; maybe we could grind that up and put it in hot water, and it would take the place of milk.

Mom was afraid it wouldn't.

I didn't have any ideas.

Frankie was squawling her head off, and it was impossible not to sympathize with her. Mom said, "Well if I write a note to Mr. Johnson will you take it down and—"

Marge and I began to whimper and whine. The boys would chase us if we went out again and we'd just break the next bottle of milk like we had the first; besides, Mr. Johnson was a mean ol' man and wouldn't trust anyone for anything. He had big signs up all over the store saying he wouldn't. "You just go down and see for yourself, Mom."

Jim Thompson

Mom said she guessed she'd have to.

We got out her old black serge dress and a shawl and some houseslippers, and Marge did the best she could with pinning up her hair. Then we wrapped Frankie up in a blanket and started out. We took Frankie because Mom wouldn't leave her alone, and she needed me and Marge to lean on.

It was bitterly cold, and I thought that was what was making Mom shiver. But it wasn't—not entirely. It was just the pain of her legs going to pieces beneath her. It was only a block to the drugstore and a block back, but, as I say, her legs weren't good to start with, and she'd just had Frankie, and she hadn't been eating right for years.

We got the milk. Johnson wouldn't have given it to us, but there was a whore and her pimp in the place—swell customers—drinking coke and paregoric, and he didn't want to show himself up for what he was. He even threw in a small bottle of soothing syrup which, no doubt, he would have had to throw out in the alley before long anyway. It had a little label under the regular one—rather, part of a label; most of it was torn off. The remaining letters read OPI—

We got back to the house, and went into the kitchen. The gas hadn't been cut off yet, although I can't figure out why. Mom put Frankie down on the table, and sat down herself; and Marge and I fixed the milk and filled the bottle. I'll swear to this day that Frankie rose up out of her blankets and snatched it from our hands.

She took a big swig, and said "Gush," and gave us a tight self-satisfied Hoover smile. Then she closed her eyes and got down to business.

Mom said, "That milk looks so good I believe I'll have some. You kids ought to drink some, too."

We kids didn't like milk. We never liked anything that was good for us, probably because we so seldom had the opportunity to acquire the liking.

"You like ice-cream sodas, don't you?" said Mom. "I could fix it so it'd be sweet and nice. You'd sleep better if you had something warm on your stomachs."

Well...an ice-cream soda—that put the matter in a different light.

We heated another pan of milk, and filled three glasses. And Mom put a third of the bottle of soothing syrup into each one. It was such a little bottle, and Mom didn't know any better. Pop said afterwards that she should have, and that Johnson ought to have been horsewhipped. But Pop wasn't there that night.

I remember, dimly, in the haze-filled passages I fled slowly through, a white face that kept rising up before me—a white face and long black hair and warning terror-stricken eyes that kept forcing themselves open with the invisible fingers of sheer will. And when I saw that face, I retreated and was somehow glad.

Once I had wandered deep along a subterranean corridor, following an odor, a sound, a vision—I do not know what it was but it was irresistible. And I had come to a carved archway, and there was a laughing little girl on the other side, holding out her hands to me. Jo. Jo holding out her hands and trying to grasp mine.

No. I mean it. It was Jo. That was more than fifteen years before Jo was born, but I knew at once that it was Jo, and she knew that I was her father.

I said, "Where's your mother?" And Jo laughed and tossed her hair, and said, "Oh, she isn't here. Come on in and play with me."

I said, "All right," and stepped toward her, and she bent her little face to kiss my hand.

And then Mom appeared between us.

She struck Jo—struck her and kept striking her. And Jo screamed at me for help, and I stood motionless and horrified, sad yet relieved. I stood there until Mom had beaten Jo to death with her bare fists. And then Mom motioned for me to precede her back up the passageway, and I obeyed. I went back up the passage, leaving Jo dead there in the little room.

Jo has never liked Mom....

There was a large white pavilion with a small circular pool. And strong hands kept pushing me toward the pool, and I did not want to go into it because it was black and bitter. I wondered why Mom didn't save me, and I cried out to her, and a dozen voices shouted back, "He's coming out of it! He's going to be all right, Mrs. Dillon...."

I opened my eyes. The black coffee rose lazily from the oil cloth and I drank. I had been asleep thirty hours, seven more than Marge. Mom had shaken off her stupor as soon as Frankie began to holler for more milk.

A few nights later Pop came home. He came in a taxicab, and it was filled with packages. He had a new coat for Mom—she hated it always and wore it about as long—a suit for me, dresses for Marge, shoes for all of us (none of them fit), toys, watches, candy, rye bread, horseradish, pigs feet, bologna—God knows what all.

Marge and I danced around Mom's bed, laughing and eating

and unwrapping things, while Mom lay there trying to smile and Pop looked on in happy pride. Then I noticed the little black grip he was carrying.

"What's in that, Pop? What else you got in that, Pop?" I yelled, Marge joining me.

Pop held the bag up over our heads and giggled. And we stopped yelling and jumping for a moment because the giggle startled us. Pop was such a big man, and so dignified even in his amusement. I think he was the only man I ever saw who could look dignified with his pants torn and chili on his vest. Pop always wore good clothes, but he was a little careless about their upkeep.

He unfastened the catch on the bag and turned it upside down, and a shower of currency, money orders, and certified checks floated down to the bed and floor.

His oil well had come in. He had already sold a fraction of his holdings for 65,000 dollars. And here it was.

The artist should have stayed for that picture, too. Mom with her legs as big and black as stovepipes, and 65,000 dollars on the bed....

Well, her legs are still like that. And Pop is still drilling oil wells—very real oil wells, to him at least. As for me—

As for me....